Puffin Books

THE DONS

Paul is trying to escape.

He's trying to escape from an Italian heritage that just doesn't seem to have relevance for him any more, and he's trying to escape from his nonno. They come from two different worlds, he and his grandfather, and Paul is more interested in his *own* world – his friends, the girls, the fast cars, the go-carts – than Nonno's strange and embarrassing behaviour.

Nonno is more than just a silly old man getting in the way of Paul's lifestyle, though. Nonno has more stories to tell than Paul can even begin to imagine. But there is one big problem – Nonno is losing his mind.

Also by Archimede Fusillo

Sparring with Shadows

ARCHIMEDE FUSILLO

THE DONS

Puffin Books

Puffin Books
Penguin Books Australia Ltd
487 Maroondah Highway, PO Box 257
Ringwood, Victoria 3134, Australia
Penguin Books Ltd
Harmondsworth, Middlesex, England
Penguin Putnam Inc.
375 Hudson Street, New York, New York 10014, USA
Penguin Books Canada Limited
10 Alcorn Avenue, Toronto, Ontario, Canada M4V 3B2
Penguin Books (NZ) Ltd
Cnr Rosedale and Airborne Roads, Albany, Auckland, New Zealand
Penguin Books (South Africa) (Pty) Ltd
24 Sturdee Avenue, Rosebank, Johannesburg 2196, South Africa
Penguin Books India (P) Ltd
11, Community Centre, Panchsheel Park, New Delhi 110 017, India

First published by Penguin Books Australia, 2001

1 3 5 7 9 10 8 6 4 2

Design and digital imaging by Ellie Exarchos
Cover photography by Theo Kinigopoulos, Getty Images and photolibrary.com
Typeset in 11.5/16 pt Janson Text by Post Pre-press Group, Brisbane, Queensland
Printed and bound in Australia by McPherson's Printing Group, Maryborough, Victoria

National Library of Australia
Cataloguing-in-Publication data:

Fusillo, Archimede.
The Dons.

ISBN 0 14 131334 X.

1. Senile dementia – Fiction. 2. Italians – Australia – Fiction. I. Title.

A823.3

www.puffin.com.au
www.penguin.com.au

Archimede wishes to thank his editor, Suzanne Wilson, for seeing amongst the debris of the earliest
draft of this novel a story worth telling, and striving to make him tell it as honestly as possible.

Every effort has been made to locate the copyright holder of the images contained in this book.
The publisher welcomes any information, and will be pleased to
make an acknowledgement in future editions.

In memory of
Nonna Maria Teresa Fusillo (1908-1991) who
was born in Viggiano, Southern Italy, and made
a home for herself in Melbourne, Australia: to
the memory of her stories, and those of like
people. They left behind everything to follow
loved ones in search of something as fragile, yet
as inspiring, as hope.

And dedicated to
Pina, my beautiful wife, who gives me unconditional
support so that I can have the freedom to write, and
my children Alyssa and Laurence, who make my
every effort worthwhile.

Old age hath yet his honour and his toil . . .
We are not now that strength which in old days
Moved earth and heaven; that which we are, we are;
One equal temper of heroic hearts,
Made weak by time and fate, but strong in will
To strive, to seek, to find, and not to yield.

'Ulysses' ALFRED, LORD TENNYSON

Sometimes I wish I could just fly away. Not for ever, just for a little while. A few years, maybe. Just until I can stop missing Dad the way everyone but Mum and Nonno say I should after five years. Maybe just until I can figure out how to keep Nonno from slipping between the present and wherever it is he goes sometimes . . .

Paul 'The Don' Taranto

1

The police have just knocked on our front door. I saw them from the window as they pulled up in their divvy van. One of them, the younger one, is rocking on the balls of his feet. He looks nervous.

I reckon they're here about the car.

My nonno went to his regular card game at the Italian Club where he gets taken three days a week, and instead of waiting for his usual lift home he's come home with a Porsche. A brand new shiny red Porsche Carrera. My nonno doesn't have a driver's licence any more. My nonno doesn't own a car. Mum doesn't know about the Porsche . . . yet.

When I asked my grandfather why he'd come home with a Porsche he told me it's because Porsches are fast and he had to get home before it started to rain.

I can understand that. The man's in his seventies and he suffers from all sorts of ailments, most of which Mum says are imaginary. But hey, Nonno is an old man and catching a cold at his age could be serious. And besides, him and me share a room and the last time he caught a cold his sniffling and coughing kept me awake for a week. I went to school looking like something the Mafia had buried for a month and forgotten about, until it came floating up out of the sewers into one of Melbourne's main streets.

Problem with Nonno's story is, it hasn't rained in Melbourne for about a month. I reckon it's going to be a long dry summer once school gets out for the Christmas break in a few weeks. Who can wait!

'What's happened? What's wrong?' Mum asks, all twitchy nervy now that I've decided to open the door and she can see the two policemen standing there.

'It's about a stolen car,' the younger of the two officers replies, adding, 'Can we come in?'

I see Mum's eyes roll in her head. It happens to her when she gets nervy, especially when the police come to the door – which isn't often I should tell you. She does it even when the Mormons or the Jehovahs come knocking. I think it's just something to do with unexpected knocks at the door. Like when the police came to tell us about Dad.

'We don't have a stolen car,' I say because I can see right away that Mum is a bit stunned.

'I'm afraid this is the address we've been given by the party concerned,' the older police officer informs us in a voice he's obviously borrowed from a gravel pit.

'Do you have any objection to us coming in for a few moments?'

'No, no, of course not. Come in.' Mum steps clear of the doorway and the two officers follow her down the hall to the kitchen.

'I have my own car. Fully paid for,' Mum offers. 'And my son Paul, well, he's almost fifteen, so . . .'

Mum! Don't you know anything about police procedure, about the law? You never offer information.

The younger police officer grins and takes out a notepad, flips it open and then blinks something from his eye.

'Is anyone else at home?' the older officer asks.

'My father, but he's asleep right now.' Mum is wiping her hands on her jeans and I can tell the younger officer is pretty impressed. Mum still has a good figure for her age.

'Could you wake him, please.' It isn't a question. The older officer isn't smiling.

Nonno is a light sleeper but it still takes him ages to get started again once he's down. I think the officers think he's done a runner when Mum comes back and tells them he'll be a few minutes and would they like a drink. A snack, maybe? What about a piece of fresh watermelon on such a warm afternoon?

If he was on his own the younger cop would have taken the lot: drink, snack and watermelon. As it is, the older cop suggests Mum please go hurry Nonno along as they have a full board of calls to make.

'So, a lot of cars get nicked today then, eh?' I try, but the older cop just gives me a freezing stare. I see the young constable's mouth turn up in a weak smile.

'Ever been in trouble with the law?' the older officer asks suddenly.

'Nup.'

'Ever done drugs?'

Is this bloke for real? I shake my head.

'You sure?'

I give the older cop a look as if to say, you reckon I'd still be standing here if I had? My mum would turn me inside out if I even went near a Panadol without written permission.

'Just checking,' the older cop adds and nods in a meaningful way at the younger cop who raises his eyebrows and forces his mouth into a tight line.

So much for positive public relations.

I'm glad when a few moments later I hear Mum and Nonno come down the hallway.

'Papa, these policemen want to talk to you,' Mum says as though she is just then breaking this bit of news to Nonno.

Nonno clucks and leans into his walking-stick. It's a sturdy, gnarled length of red gum. He made it himself years before and he topped it with the carving of a wild boar's head. Nonno says it reminds him of when he was young and would roam the woods around Monte

Sereno, his little village in southern Italy, chasing wild boars in the snow.

It's strange how Nonno can remember even the smallest details about how he would stalk a boar for hours and hours on his own, but he can't tell me who won the footy last week.

The older police officer points Nonno to a sofa, then sits down in the chair closest to him.

Nonno rubs the end of his nose.

'Does he speak English?' the older officer asks Mum over Nonno's shoulder.

Nonno looks back at Mum and purses his lips. 'You tell to him I speak the Inglish much more better than wot him speaks the Italian,' Nonno says deadpan, then turns back to face the officer.

I see the older cop stiffen. He clears his throat and sniffs heavily. The younger officer scratches his left ear and looks down at his feet.

'Do you know anything about a missing Porsche?' the older cop asks. 'A red Porsche?'

'A *Porsche*!' Mum exclaims. 'What Porsche?'

Mum looks directly at me as though *I* would know. I do, but I don't say anything. I was hoping no one would notice.

'It wos look like him come to rain,' Nonno says slowly. 'I wos go play cards and it was clean sky. No cloud. When I start come home I see it many clouds.' Nonno raises a knobbly hand towards the window, encouraging the police officer in front of him to turn and look for himself.

'I not want get wet,' Nonno continues. 'Best way not get wet is hiave own car.'

'Didn't you get a lift as usual today?' Mum cuts in with real surprise. She looks at me. 'Paul, didn't your nonno come home on the bus with the others?'

I swallow but don't commit to anything.

The older cop coughs and looks at me and Mum in turn. He leans closer to Nonno. Nonno leans in towards the older cop. 'I'll ask you again. Did you take a red Porsche from the . . .' He consults his notepad. 'The . . .' He obviously can't pronounce the name so he just says, '. . . the Italian Club here in Brunswick?'

Nonno rubs his chin, chews his gums and sits back on the sofa. 'Porsche is good car for young peoples,' he says. 'Too fast for the old mans.'

'So you admit to driving a Porsche from the Club?' the older cop presses.

'But you can't drive, Papa,' Mum says.

'I not say enniting about me *drive*,' Nonno answers, waving away Mum's concern. 'I joust says I wos tink him comes rain and car is good for not get wet.'

Mum rubs her forehead. Her eyes narrow. I cover my mouth with my hand. This should be good.

'Porsche she is fast car,' Nonno goes on. 'Fast car can get me to home quicker than slow car.' He smiles and shrugs. 'I old but I not completely stupid.' He

6

turns and looks at me and grins. 'True or no?' he asks me. I nod.

'So you admit to taking the car?' The older cop's voice is straining a little now.

Mum steps up and puts a hand on Nonno's shoulder. 'He's an old man,' she snaps and I can see she is a bit lost at this point. 'What would an old man want with a Porsche?' Then a moment later adds, 'How could my father steal a car? He can't drive!'

'Where's the car now?' The older cop ignores Mum. The younger cop smiles at her. I give him a dirty, then tap Nonno on the shoulder.

'You don't have to say anything,' I cut in, then to the older policeman, 'Unless you're under arrest for something.' I watch enough cop shows on TV to know that everyone has a right to remain silent. Anything you say, can and will . . .

Nonno touches the side of his nose. It's the code sign we use to each other when playing cards as a team, to signal that we have a good hand.

'In my room,' he says softly through a cheery grin. 'On the wardrobe.'

Mum frowns. It is the older cop's turn to scratch his head.

'Can we see it?' asks the younger cop.

Without a word Nonno gets up and shuffles out of the kitchen.

'He's not what he was,' Mum says under her breath,

her voice weary all of a sudden. 'You can see that. A Porsche on the wardrobe . . .' She tries to smile but her face deflates like a left-over party balloon.

The older cop isn't listening, anyway. He follows Nonno down the hallway. And we follow him in turn.

'You see,' Nonno beams when we enter the cramped bedroom he and I share. 'I not even scratch her one little bit.' And Nonno holds out for the older police officer to take a scale model of a Porsche Carrera, still boxed.

'Better if she wos Ferrari!' Nonno says. 'Ferrari Italiano. Ferrari can leave Porsche in the dust wot they say.'

I want to laugh. So does the young constable. I see him rub his hand across his mouth. He's looking at my mum a lot I notice. Maybe he thinks we're a model-car stealing syndicate or something, and Mum is the supremo.

'Is this a joke?' the older cop asks shortly. He shoves the Porsche back at Nonno. Nonno takes it and I see the thinnest grin on his face.

It takes some sweet talk from Mum, but finally she manages to make the older officer see the funny side of the sad situation. I mean, he should have worked it out for himself. How could an old man in his seventies nick a Porsche? A real Porsche, anyway. It's all a mis-understanding. Nonno didn't steal a real Porsche. He didn't even steal the model Porsche. Not really.

'He probably just got confused,' Mum explains when we are all back in the kitchen. 'He usually gets a lift home from the Club. My dad probably just got confused when he thought it would rain and wandered off looking for a way to get home without getting wet. The Porsche is probably part of the prizes they're collecting for the Christmas raffle.'

'But we had a report that a Porsche had been stolen from the premises,' the older cop tells Mum.

Mum threads an arm through Nonno's. She pats his shoulder gently. Nonno smiles at her. 'You'll most likely find the report was made by one of my father's friends.' Mum lowers her voice, but she can't disguise the sadness there. 'A lot of them at the Club are like my father. Someone must have seen Dad walking out with the car, told someone else, and before you know it . . . Chinese whispers, you know. The real message got scrambled.'

I listen to Mum, but I watch Nonno. He's not smiling or frowning. He's just there, waiting. It reminds me of what happened a few weeks earlier when Nonno was sitting on the front porch and calling to our neighbours across the road that they should do something about their personal hygiene. Nonno said they had all started reeking lately and the stench was putting him off his food. Coming home with the model Porsche, that was just another of those things Nonno does occasionally that sends Mum into a bit of a spin – even though she knows Nonno doesn't mean any harm by what he does.

The older officer clears his throat a lot as he explains to Mum that they have an obligation to investigate apparently legitimate reports about theft, and I can see that he finds it all as embarrassing as Mum does. After all, Nonno explained that he was going to return the car when the weather improved.

'I not want keep him,' Nonno says about a hundred times as the older officer tries to make him understand that Nonno could get himself into trouble if he doesn't take a little more care.

Nonno shakes his head, his eyes downcast. He refuses to say any more. Even when the younger cop tells Nonno that they'll sort out the confusion, Nonno just stares at the floor.

'You're lucky they didn't force my hand and have you locked away,' Mum says in exasperation once the police officers have left, and hands Nonno a bag of pistachio nuts from a kitchen cupboard.

'One day you'll go too far and then I won't have a choice,' Mum adds. But she says no more because something gets stuck in her throat at this point. Maybe it's the pistachio nut Nonno shelled and insisted she have.

'Ah, they make the fuss,' Nonno tells me as I help him out of his waistcoat. 'So a man him gets old. It happen. You not can blame him for hims age . . .'

'Guess you can't,' I try because we've had this

discussion maybe a hundred times before. I've lost count of how many times Nonno and I have sat in the bedroom we share and I've tried to make him see that not everyone appreciates his odd sense of humour.

'But I not go be locked up like dog wot wait to die!' he snaps and touches the side of his nose again.

I shake my head. 'No one's gonna lock you up, Nonno,' I say because it's what he needs to hear. And because despite all the grief he gives me sometimes, I couldn't bear to think of my nonno in a home.

Inside though, I know Mum can't go on for ever the way she has since Dad died. Nonno is getting just a little too difficult to take sometimes, even for me, and I don't have to clean up after him the way Mum does.

2

Mum is fuming. 'Last week your nonno comes home with a rake he says he found on a vacant block, but later it turns out to be from the Henesseys' garden up the road. He just saw it there on the lawn and thought he could help himself to it. *Why?* Because "these Australians not know how to till the soil and it would be a waste to leave such a useful tool lying around like that".' Mum waves her dishcloth at me and sighs. 'And today he comes home with a *Porsche*!'

I'm tossing cutlery into the drawer as fast as I can because I have to get out before it gets dark. Mum hates it when I toss stuff. She reckons it shows disrespect for the hard work that has gone into getting the money to buy the stuff in the first place. I don't have time to think about respect right now. I have to see Tracey Reynolds.

'There was a time when your nonno was as sharp as a pin,' Mum says. 'He had a real head for figures . . .

and music.' Mum lowers her voice. 'Nonno had a magnificent voice as a boy, did you know that? I've never heard him, of course. Says he can't remember how to sing.' Mum chuckles. 'Hasn't forgotten how to play that piano accordion though, has he?'

I switch off. I know the story backwards: if only Nonno had not been born into a poor peasant family he might have been able to cultivate his mind. If only Nonno hadn't been born into a tiny village full of goat and sheep herders, he might have been able to get a proper education and have made something of his life.

Mum likes to use Nonno as a kind of role model for me – especially since Dad died, to make me realise how important it is I get a good education. Nonno reckons he never needed a formal education. Nonno reckons he got all the education he needed from trying to survive.

But I can't tell Mum that. It would break her heart. She thinks I'm going to 'grow up' and become a doctor or a lawyer.

Dream on.

You know what I really want to do? I want to drive Formula 1 cars. I want to drive Formula 1 cars and be an Australian Formula 1 ace. That's what I want to do. Mum doesn't know it maybe, but Formula 1 drivers make heaps of money. Some of them even get to fly their very own jets and helicopters. I could buy myself a fleet of cars and house them in purpose-built climate-controlled garages.

I can see it so clearly. Being able to buy Mum her very own sports convertible complete with a twelve-stack CD player and high-tech satellite navigation system. Mum'd never get lost again. And even if she did manage to lose herself (like she did just last week when instead of driving out to Chadstone she found herself in Chelsea) she could listen to music in air-conditioned comfort until help arrived.

But I can't tell Mum that right now. Right now Mum is more concerned with Nonno's weird behaviour, and the fact that I've failed three of the last four science tests. I don't usually do too badly at school, but lately my mind hasn't been on study. My mind's been on Tracey Reynolds.

'The Henesseys said Nonno did them a favour by taking the rake,' I put in, to show that I have heard some of what Mum said. If I don't she's likely to get me to repeat her entire spiel.

'Mrs Henessey reckons they were going to throw that old rake out, anyway.'

Mum stops rubbing the pattern off one of the dinner plates and looks at me. 'That's not the point, Paul. The point is that your nonno should never have taken it in the first place. I don't know what gets into his head sometimes . . .'

Just then Nonno shuffles in. He's been at the toilet. I can tell because he has the ends of his shirt sticking out of his fly.

Mum spots it and groans.

'It's a boy thing, Ma,' I say and try to get Nonno to tuck himself in. He fidgets and makes it difficult for me to get a grip on the zip, but finally I manage to get him looking respectable.

'Imagine if those policemen were still here and you walked out looking like that,' Mum says with a forced laugh. We both see that Nonno is a little embarrassed by his oversight.

'I'm sorry, Teresa,' Nonno whispers in Mum's direction and I have to get out of his way quick because he's decided he needs to give Mum a hug. He crashes his walking-stick into the furniture as he crosses the kitchen and pats Mum lightly on the shoulder before giving her a gentle squeeze.

I see Mum's shoulders heave and decide that it's a good time to exit.

'Where're you off to?' Mum calls.

'Out!' I shout back because I heard someone on TV shout that back at their mum and I liked the way it sort of made the kid's mum roll her eyes in amusement.

I don't know if Mum rolled her eyes in amusement or not but I hear her words as I fly out of the shed on my bike: 'Don . . . e . . . ome . . . ate . . . erstand?'

By the time I hit the street all I hear is my own mind ticking over. Please God, let Tracey be at the track, please.

I ride with my head down, pumping the pedals hard, my arse up in the air.

Tracey Reynolds is the hottest babe ever to enrol at Northern High. She only started last term but already she's made a name for herself as the most drop-dead gorgeous chick in Year 10. I mean, this girl has style. Tracey Reynolds lived on the Gold Coast before coming down to Melbourne so she's got the most fantastic suntan. She's pretty radical, too. No other girl in our class has ever thought to turn up at school wearing one set of clothes and leave in another. At lunchtime Tracey changes from what she calls her a.m. clothes into her p.m. clothes.

So cool. So out there.

No wonder the other chicks are drooling envy every time Tracey is within sight of them. Tracey makes them all look like ferals.

I round the final bend towards the school running track and screech to a halt a respectable distance from where I figure Tracey should be.

I wish I had the guts to just walk out and announce myself to her. *Hey, hiya Tracey. Paul Taranto. Yeah, that's right, I'm in your homeroom class. Well, thanks. Sure, sometimes I do get stopped and mistaken for . . . Sorry? You thought I was too cool for you to approach. Tracey, no. You shouldn't feel threatened by my charm . . .*

Not exactly how the conversation would run, but it'll do for me for now. Until I do get to talk to her . . .

Dan Declan reckons Tracey gave him a wink yesterday after PE. I reckon Tracey got a bit of mascara in her eye. Dan's been my mate since for ever and I reckon I can trust him, though I haven't really let on too much about Tracey yet. I don't want to be hassled if things don't work out between me and Tracey, especially since Tracey doesn't know about me and her being an item yet.

Dan reckons Tracey is a wanna-be. I reckon I wanna be wherever she is. Especially over the summer break when she'll probably get down to the local pool like everyone else.

Dan reckons Tracey is up herself. I reckon Dan should get his hand off it before he goes blind.

I spot Tracey and push Dan out of my mind. Tracey's doing stretches and squats. She's an athlete. She runs most Sundays during the aths season. She trains for hours and hours after school with her dad who's also her coach.

I know all this because I've made it my business to be informed. Yeah.

'Getting a good perv, Taranto?' It's Dan.

I try not to look startled but I step back from my perch behind a tall hedge too quickly.

Dan laughs. 'Knew you had the hots for her all along,' he smirks.

'Yeah, right,' I say back at him. 'As if.'

'She's cute,' Dan adds as though he hasn't heard me. 'Cute in a stuck up sort of way.'

I try to find something on my bike to take some interest in. I fiddle with the rear pegs and shake the chain, grip and feel the tension on the brakes. And all the time Dan watches me with a grin on his stupid face.

'You spoken to her yet or what?'

'Maybe.'

'Yeah, sure,' Dan gushes. 'Didn't think so.' I feel rather than see Dan laugh under his breath. If he wasn't my best mate I'd probably deck him.

'Paul, we've been mates a long time,' Dan adds. 'I can pick it when a chick's got your engine pumping. You reckon I don't see you sneaking a peek at her in class?'

'What are you doing here, anyway?' I ask, looking for a way to change the topic.

'Karate!' Dan says and goes into a kung-fu stance.

Shit. I'd forgotten. Dan has karate classes in the school hall one night a week. Just my luck it had to be tonight.

Dan looks past me towards Tracey. I follow his gaze.

'She's got a nice bod, I'll give her that much,' Dan says slowly. 'Maybe I should just call her over . . .'

When Dan cups his hands over his mouth as though he's about to yell out to Tracey, I shove him in the chest. He laughs and shakes his head.

'Sad,' he says. 'Tracey Reynolds of all people. She's about as stuck up as you can get, Taranto.'

I swing onto my bike and lean back, arms folded, face set blank. 'Thought I'd done a sprocket,' I say as deadpan as possible. 'I felt the front wheel vibrate.'

Dan laughs. 'The front wheel, you reckon,' he sneers. 'Sure it wasn't your own suspension?'

'You're sick, Declan,' I answer quickly. I think about sneaking another glance at Tracey Reynolds over Dan's shoulder but decide not to risk it.

'She's not your *type*, Taranto,' Dan scoffs now that he seems to have regained control over his laughing fit. 'She hasn't got a moustache for a start. And besides, her old man's a councillor and he wouldn't want his little girl going out with the grandson of a car thief.'

'What?'

Dan shuffles. He picks up his sports bag and grins. 'What?' he says, mimicking me.

'You're full of it tonight, Declan,' I spit, annoyed more about Dan turning up than anything he might know about Nonno.

'The word's getting out there, Taranto,' Dan explains dramatically. 'You forget mate, my nextdoor neighbour runs the kitchen at that wog club, remember? Not much happens there that she doesn't know about.'

'Shit!'

'Yeah, shit, eh,' Dan grins. 'Seems some old codger nicked a Porsche from the club and did a runner. Cops got called in and all, eh. Mrs Santos was telling Mum all about it. She reckons your grandad was cool *as*. He just headed off with the Porsche like it was his.'

I look at Dan. He quits grinning and stares back at me, hard.

'Nonno just gets confused sometimes,' I say.

For a few moments we just stare at each other. I can feel my insides go soft. I hate it when Nonno embarrasses Mum and me like this, especially with my mates. And lately he just seems to do it more and more often.

'He never stole the Porsche,' I begin. 'It was a misunderstanding. Nonno's harmless.'

Dan winks at me. 'Yeah, right, harmless,' he grins. 'I reckon your grandfather's one of them Don blokes. Like they have in those gangster films . . .' Dan squares his shoulders and narrows his eyes. 'I'm gonna make youse an offer youse can't refuse, punk!' he warbles in his Mafia voice and breaks up laughing again.

'You're a comedian, Dan Declan,' I throw back at him. 'You should have your own TV show.'

Dan shakes his head. 'Hey, all I'm saying is that Tracey's old man won't ever agree to his daughter going out with the nephew of a Don, you know. And she's a super spunk, right? So, why would she go out with you?'

I look at Dan. He's not trying to be a smartarse. Well, maybe just a little bit. Dan's right, though. Tracey Reynolds is a super spunk. There's no way she's ever going to be interested in a guy whose Nonno is a car thief. And even if she is, Declan is right again, her old man would go ballistic.

And then it occurs to me . . .

If Dan Declan knows about Nonno already, then who else does?

I'm about to ask Dan what else he knows when he nods for me to look behind me. I do, and see Tracey Reynolds heading off the track towards the change rooms.

'Missed your shot, Lover Boy,' Dan teases. I give him the finger. He gives it right back to me.

'Hey, that's all crap about me liking Tracey, okay,' I say without too much conviction. 'You're right, she's not my type and . . .'

I don't have to finish. Dan nods his head slowly.

'And your bike burst a sprocket,' he says cagily. 'I know. I've burst a few myself . . . If you know what I mean.'

I shake my head. Some mate.

'You done that English assignment on oral histories yet or what?' I ask, because I really don't want to talk about Tracey Reynolds or my nonno any more for the time being. Both are giving me grief right now.

Dan screws up his mouth. 'What's to do?' he says off-handedly. 'I've probably failed English, anyway.'

I look at my watch. I won't be expected home again for at least another hour or so.

'Burger?' I ask. 'My shout.'

Dan looks a little surprised. He pats his flat belly. 'I'm in training,' he says seriously, then adds, 'Will there be fries with that?'

I nod. I just want to get away from here. I've missed any chance I might have had of approaching Tracey for tonight.

'Hey, Taranto,' Dan says as he walks beside me. 'Reckon Don Nonno can get my old lady a new Commodore Series II Sportspak? It's her birthday tomorrow and I haven't bought her anything yet.'

I give Dan the finger again.

Sometimes I wish I'd been born into a family of hermits, well away from normal people with normal everyday lives. Well away from old men like my nonno who dribble at the dinner table and steal toy cars and call your mum by their dead wife's name. Maybe even away from girls like Tracey Reynolds who'll never look twice at someone who has to share a bedroom with an old man.

3

I almost don't walk into the kitchen when I get home. I almost turn and jump back on my bike and pedal off to join a religious sect. One that doesn't mind having kids in it who have visions about selling their nonno off to a band of wandering buskers.

Take him, I'd say. My nonno can draw a crowd just by standing in the middle of a busy street and quoting from the Bible. I know because he did it once in the Bourke Street Mall while Mum and I popped into Myers so I could buy a new pair of jeans. He was supposed to have been waiting quietly for us on one of the benches, eating his pistachio nuts and watching the crowd.

I almost ride off but decide I can't keep avoiding my aunty Rita, or Zia as she prefers me to call her. I can hear her voice as I come up the drive.

Zia Rita is Mum's sister. She's not married. Well, she was, once or twice. She lives not far from us but far enough away, Mum reckons, so that Zia Rita doesn't have to share the responsibility over Nonno.

She and Mum get along okay though, especially when they're apart.

'Well, look who's here!' Zia Rita exclaims when I walk in.

'Who?' I say and look around.

She laughs. 'You're getting more handsome every time I see you. Isn't he, Teresa?'

Mum mumbles something. I think it's, *What would you know, you stupid cow. You only ever come here when you need something.* But I can't be certain because Nonno is sitting at the kitchen table playing his piano accordion.

'Great tune there, Nonno,' I tell him and toss my shoes into the laundry. Not that it is. Not for me, anyway. It's the same old umpa-umpa tune he plays when the mood takes him, or when he remembers he can play the piano accordion.

Nonno doesn't seem to have heard me. What is it with people not hearing me when I talk to them? Nonno is smiling alternatively at the ceiling and then down at his slippers.

'Have the TV news crews come round yet?' I ask Mum.

She frowns.

'What, Nonno hasn't made the late news?' I shake my head in mock disappointment.

'TV crews?' Zia Rita is doing her impression of a

Barbie doll. You know the type, sweeps back her hair when she speaks, her hands all fluttery. Mum reckons her sister has a nervous condition. I just reckon Zia Rita *is* a condition.

'You tinks they put me on the televish?' Nonno looks straight at me. He can hear pretty well when he wants to.

'I tinks they put you in orbit,' I say, then more quietly add, 'You're out there, anyway.' Mum must have heard because she gives me a greasy and asks if I've done my English homework. I don't answer. Sometimes it's better that way. Keeps Mum on her toes.

'So, you all set for Saturday then, Paul?' Zia Rita asks because obviously she's got no interest in what happened to Nonno earlier today. And as Mum would say, why should she when Mum's around to do all the worrying.

'What's Saturday?'

Zia Rita does a heave and looks shocked. 'Saturday. You know!'

I look at Mum for help. She stares back at me.

'Can't be the footy,' I try, ''cause the footy season's over. And it can't be cricket because you never come to any matches I play, anyway.' I shake my head. 'Sorry, can't help you.'

'You promised to help me with the garage sale! Remember?'

'Why for you sell you garage?' Nonno pipes up. 'Is still good. Wot for you sell him?'

'Take a reality check, Nonno,' I tell him, in the nicest way I can. I can do that sometimes, get Nonno back on track. Sharing a bedroom with Nonno means I've had to learn to read the signs that tell me when he's about to go into no-man's-land. Like in the middle of the night when he wakes me to tell me we have to go check on the sheep. It's my job to get Nonno back into bed as quickly and quietly as possible. I don't want to have to keep waking Mum. She worries enough about Nonno already.

'Is the garage sale *this* week?' I say and bite my bottom lip. I'd forgotten all about it, actually. In fact, I'd made plans to go go-carting with Dan. 'Gee, eh . . .' I look at Mum. 'This Saturday, eh . . .'

But Mum doesn't bite and turns away. She's always on at me about being responsible for my actions. I've made my zia a promise, not that I remember making it of course, and now I'm stuck with it. At least as far as Mum is concerned, anyway. Good one! What with Nonno and now the garage sale, when am I supposed to do anything about me and Tracey Reynolds?

'Of course it's *this* Saturday. That's what I've put on all the signs and things.' Zia presses her fingertips to her mouth as though she might say a prayer. 'I thought maybe you could sleep over on Friday night, Paul. That way you can give me a hand to sort out the last-minute bits and pieces, and you can be there bright and early with me when the first buyers roll up on Saturday morning. What do you think, Teresa?'

Mum grins and presses her tongue into the side of her mouth. 'I think that's one of your more sensible ideas, Rita.'

'Good.'

Zia Rita smiles at me and I smile back thinly – total frustration or what!

Even if Dan is right and Tracey isn't my type, I figure it's still worth a try. This garage sale is the last thing I need on the weekend.

'What about cricket, Mum?' I say even though cricket training doesn't start for another few weeks yet, not for my lowly team anyway. 'You know I have cricket practice Saturday mornings. I can't let the boys down!'

'So did *you* when you made Zia the promise,' Mum answers and I know there's just no way she is going to let me wriggle out of this one.

'Bloody cricket,' Nonno snipes suddenly. 'Wot game is dis? Grown man stand with stick in him hands and try hit bloody ball!'

'Yeah well, what about soccer? You aren't even allowed to use your hands unless you're the goalie. Get serious, Nonno. You can't call soccer a real ball game!'

Nonno dismisses me with a wave of his hand and starts up the music again. Cricket is another thing we can never agree on. He hates it. I love it. Nonno loves getting up in the middle of the night and talking about whatever gets into his head: I like sleeping. He likes pistachio nuts: I like donuts.

'What're you going to do with Nonno?' I ask Mum. 'You're working this Saturday morning, aren't you?' I'm hoping Mum has just forgotten. She usually leaves Nonno with me for a few hours on the odd Saturday when she does have to go into the dry cleaners. That's where she works, permanent part-time. If I'm playing cricket or footy I just rug Nonno up and take him along, sit him on the sidelines and keep an eye on him.

'I'll drop him off to you both on my way to work,' she answers simply, as though this had all been planned well ahead of time. 'That way he won't be in the way while you set up . . .'

I can see Zia Rita isn't keen on the idea. She's twisted her Barbie mouth into a zigzag line.

Mum notices. 'What do you expect me to do with him, Rita? Take him to work with me?'

'Can you?'

Mum and I both look at her together.

'What?' she whimpers.

4

'Garage sale?' Dan laughs right into my face. 'You're gonna give up the chance to race because of a bloody garage sale. Tell me I didn't hear right.'

Thanks for the support, I think and flop into my desk.

'What, you trying to raise money so you can take Tracey out on a hot date?' Dan laughs again, only this time he thumps my desk and draws everyone's attention. 'Why don't you just get The Don to nick another Porsche and then you can on-sell it at a profit . . .'

'He's not The Don,' I say calmly.

Dan pulls a face. 'I'm gonna make youse an offer you can't refuse,' he says in his Mafia voice again.

Funny, ha, ha.

Well, at least Dan Declan thinks his joke is funny. He's laughing so hard the veins in his temples are about to burst. I look around: no one bothers with Dan when he cracks it like this. They've learnt to ignore him.

'You can't back out now, Taranto,' he says once he's over his amusement. 'There's three to a team, and me, you and Bahmir are it.'

'Look, I'm real sorry, but I just can't get out of it.'

Dan sits on my desk. 'Course you can, Taranto. Especially if I told you that Tracey is going to be there . . .'

I look up, too quickly.

'Yeah, thought that might have an impact.' Dan leans into me. I can smell his breakfast: eggs and cheese.

'Given as how Tracey's got in with Magda and her crowd, and given as how Magda is going out with Bahmir, the girls thought they might come along and watch.'

I swallow hard. I can see Tracey on the far side of the classroom. She's in a deep and meaningful with Magda even as I sit watching her. Tracey looks spectacular, her hair cropped and chopped and coloured three shades of red, her face so small and perfectly oval, her . . .

'Could be your big chance, Taranto. Could be your one and only chance.' Dan pulls a frown and then looks over his shoulder at Tracey and the others. 'Who knows,' he whispers, 'Tracey might just go for a guy whose sprockets go without warning while he's perving on her.'

He jumps off my desk and laughs at the top of his

voice but I still manage to land a punch, knocking over my desk and the books on the desk in the next row.

'Cretin!' I yell before I can stop myself.

'*Mr* Taranto!'

Lady Fang, also known as Miss Wildermere, our homeroom and English teacher, snaps my name and the entire classroom falls silent. She's just waltzed in and is glaring at me from the doorway.

I give Dan a dirty and then turn to face Lady Fang.

I can feel the eyes of the class on me, especially those beautiful hazel eyes of Tracey's. Soft, doe eyes that . . .

'Recess today, Mr Taranto,' Lady Fang announces without ceremony. 'You can come to the staffroom and collect a rubbish bag and gloves. Then, since you seem so good at creating a mess, I'd like to see how good you are at cleaning up the main oval. Is that clear?'

I nod. I can just imagine what a complete dork I look like right now.

Dan reaches out and tugs at my windcheater. 'One and only chance, Taranto,' he whispers and instinctively I make a move to push his hand away. Sprung!

'And you, Mr Declan, can help him.'

Dan splutters and I hear a titter of laughter from the rest of the class. When I look up I see Tracey shaking her head, but whether it's at me or Dan I can't tell.

'Thanks for nothing, Taranto,' Dan says when Lady Fang turns away.

'Like it was my fault,' I snap but all that does is get Lady Fang's back up even more and she fixes me with her beady eyes.

'Perhaps you might care to come back Saturday morning, Mr Taranto, and help with the clean-out of the science block as well,' she says as though this is something I really might look forward to.

Tracey is looking at me now, and there's a smirk on her face.

I don't know why but I find myself smiling at her.

'You think it's all a joke, do you, Mr Taranto?'

'What?'

'Pardon?'

'What?'

Dan laughs and pulls me down into my desk.

Tracey Reynolds rolls her eyes and I feel my face go fireball red.

'You girls there,' Lady Fang says. 'Maybe you'd all like to give those two boys a hand at recess.'

Magda does her innocent pout and Lady Fang shakes her head as though she's totally confused or uncertain, or both.

'Recess, you boys. And don't be late,' Lady Fang sneers just as the bell goes to signal first class – PE, out in the Quad.

We rush out. Lady Fang screeches that we should leave in an orderly fashion. Dan and I let everyone else go ahead of us once we're in the corridor so we can hang back and peep into the other classes as we pass.

Word's out that there's an emergency teacher in food tech today so, as we pass the food tech lab, Dan and I knock and enter.

It's a Year 8 class.

'Can I help you boys?' the emergency teacher asks when Dan and I stand there in the open doorway, staring.

It's no one we recognise so Dan starts his spiel.

'Sorry to interrupt, but could you please ask the class if anyone here has seen my friend's pet Italian carpet snake? He brought it in for biology class and it seems to have escaped from his bag.'

Dan's voice is laced with sincerity and concern. He stands looking right at the ET, one hand against his chest as though he's feeling his heartbeat.

'Italian carpet snake?' The ET looks a little uncertain. The ET is looking a little like the alien of the same name.

Dan raises his voice slightly and takes another step into the room. 'Yeah,' he says. 'An Italian carpet *snake*, about so-o long!' He places his hands about a metre apart. 'It was supposed to be for our biology class but it's got away somehow.'

There's mumbling now amongst the Year 8s. They're looking around. One or two are shuffling uneasily.

The ET looks a bit nervous.

'There's no carpet snake in here!' she says dismis-
sively. 'Who are you boys? What are your names?'

'If anyone does see it,' Dan continues, totally ignor-
ing the ET, 'could they please return it to . . .'

I hit my cue perfectly. 'What's that?' I say, pointing
towards the other side of the room over by the ovens.

I see the ET look around. The Year 8s shuffle even
more. Someone gives a yelp.

'I see it,' says Dan. 'Over there!' He points and we
both squint, hunching over. 'There by the ovens.'

'Look here,' the ET starts, but is cut off when Dan
pipes in with, 'Nah, that's not it. That's just a mouldy
length of spaghetti.'

We both look right at the ET and then I add, 'Sorry
about that, but I'm always confusing Italian carpet
snakes with mouldy lengths of spaghetti.'

We laugh and bolt, leaving the emergency teacher
floundering long enough for us to get lost amongst the
PE class out on the Quad.

One day they'll write a book about this school, and
Dan and I will be listed under the title 'Legends'. Dan
keeps reminding me of that every time he has an idea
and I seem to hesitate about seeing it through.

I like the idea of being a legend. Especially since I'll
never make it onto the honour role at this place.

Right now, though, I'd probably settle for having
Tracey Reynolds scrawl my name all over her books,
the way Magda has Bahmir's. *Magda for Bahmir.*

Bahmir is a spunk! Bahmir is a tongue lizard. Bahmir is dreamy. Bahmir ... Bahmir ...

Wonder if I should tell Tracey about the carpet snake stunt.

5

'If I have to sign another one of these forms, Paul, I swear I'll have you shipped out to a boarding school in your nonno's village back in Campagna.'

Mum has a problem with detention forms. This is the fifth one this term for me. It's sort of becoming a weekly ritual. Seems the ET didn't take kindly to the Italian carpet snake.

'They don't have boarding schools in Monte Sereno,' I try. 'I don't reckon they have regular schools even.'

'Then I'll pack you off to one run by the Vatican,' Mum grimaces. 'Then you'll see how far you get with your nonsense. You and Dan, both.'

'They won't take Dan,' I smirk. 'He's not a wog.'

Nonno is slurping his broth and I whisper to him that Mum is thinking of sending me to join the Vatican.

'They might even make me a Pope, Nonno,' I tell him and pull a serious Pope-like face. 'My first decree as Pope Aussie the First is that the members of the Carlton Football Team should all be given special dispensation to banish all future Collingwood players to hell for their heathen ways.'

Nonno sits back in his chair and wipes his chin on the tablecloth. 'I could have been a Pope,' he announces in Italian while prodding at his left ear with the end of a toothpick. 'But there was a conspiracy to keep me from being Pope. People were jealous.'

I smile at Nonno. When he talks Italian all the clumsiness is gone. His words flow. He makes sense – well, almost always. And somehow that makes what's happening to him seem even worse.

'Papa,' Mum replies in Italian, too. 'You never even went to church when you were a young man. You don't even go to church now.'

'You see?' Nonno snaps. 'Just because a man doesn't follow the herd he can't be Pope.'

'You have to be a priest first, work your way along the line of succession,' Mum adds, but doesn't go any further because there's no point.

'But Paul is not a priest,' Nonno adds. 'So why are you sending him to the Vatican to be Pope?'

I narrow my eyes. 'Yeah, Mum, why are you sending me to the Vatican?'

Mum grumbles and turns away, tossing the notice that explains why I've been given detention into the air.

Things are hard for Mum sometimes. I know that. Ever since Dad died five years ago she's had to cope with looking after me and Nonno on her own. And that can't be easy. Mum and me hardly even *ever* talk about Dad any more. We start sometimes. Mum and me start to remember things out loud, and then we sort of look at each other and stop. I see the tears in her eyes and tell her she needs to lighten up. She hiccups and tells me she loves me and then turns away.

'You want me to take Nonno for a walk?' I ask her, but the moment I say it like that, I regret the words. It sounds like Nonno is a pet that has to be exercised. 'I mean, do you want us to get out of the house for a while?'

'No,' Mum answers after what seems like ages but is probably just a few seconds. 'I'd like you to go do your homework.'

Nonno takes out his tobaccoless pipe and chews on the end of it out of habit. 'Don't take up smoking,' he advises me in his dialect and holds the pipe out at arm's length. 'If I didn't smoke when I was young I'd live to be an old man.'

'You *are* an old man,' I tell him quietly, but Mum's sagging shoulders have somehow punched a hole in the air and it's raining in the kitchen.

I go do my homework.

I go do my homework but I just sit there in the bedroom I share with Nonno and stare at the floor. I think about Mum and Nonno, and about how Mum hasn't got much of a life any more, what with having to care for her dad and me, and look after the house, and work at the dry cleaners.

One day, when I'm a wealthy Formula 1 racing ace, I'm going to buy a mansion where Mum can have her own private space away from Nonno and me, and where Nonno can have his very own bocce court. And a cards room where he can have his mates over for all-night sessions of Briscola without Mum having to worry about what he might be up to.

And I'll have a helipad right outside my front door. I'll be able to take Tracey on a sightseeing flight over my private estate, complete with exotic zoo, go-cart track and even a landing strip for my Lear jet.

This can all be yours to share with me, Tracey Reynolds, if you just don't ignore me. Otherwise, though I'd be happy to show you over the place, I'm afraid there'd be no room for you in my hectic life. Sorry! And besides, I wouldn't be able to settle down. Think about all the female fans. My being married would cause them to go into hysterics!

Nonno walks in but I don't hear him until he's right by my desk and I snap out of my daydream.

'Someones call to you on the telephone,' he tells me without ceremony.

I nod. It's probably Dan wanting to see how Mum took the news of the detention. He copped one too, but on a different day, so that we won't see the detention as a chance to muck around again, I guess. Teachers are pretty shrewd that way sometimes.

'You're not supposed to answer the phone,' I remind Nonno, remembering the time he told Zia Rita down the line that there was no one named Teresa at this number, and he'd never heard of a Paul Taranto. I feel sick deep down when I remember stuff like that.

'I forget,' Nonno whispers through a thin grin. 'I old. I forget.' He shrugs.

'Yeah, right.' Sometimes I wish I could forget, too.

When Nonno remains standing there beside my desk I try waving him away. I've got about a zillion pages of English short-answer questions to answer and I've no idea where to begin. If I had a computer I might have been able to get on the Net and find the info without having to wade through a thousand pages of Lady Fang's notes. But we can't afford a computer. Mum doesn't say so, but I reckon having Nonno in the house saps any extra money she might have been able to put away. Pity Zia Rita doesn't seem to think she needs to contribute to Nonno's upkeep.

'You want something else?' I ask.

Nonno shrugs.

'Okay then, see ya.'

'A ghel him rings on the phone,' he begins. 'She say to me want talk to you. I tell to her you busy, yes?'

I drop my pen. 'A girl? When?'

Nonno nods towards the hallway.

I jump out of my chair.

'She waiting,' Nonno smiles and gives me a sly wink. 'When I wos you age me hiave too many ghels all time want talk wit me. But not joust talk . . .'

I leave Nonno to his fantasies, run into the hall and lurch towards the phone. I pick up the receiver and lean against the wall.

'Hello?'

'Paul? Paul Taranto?'

'Yeah.'

Silence.

I see Mum's faint silhouette behind the glass of the kitchen door.

'Hi.'

The voice on the other end doesn't give me much to go on.

'Yeah, hi.'

Mum's shadow moves away.

Nonno is whistling in our bedroom. Probably messing up all my homework, too. He likes to examine things.

'Paul Taranto, right?'

'Who is this?'

'I'm calling for a friend,' the female voice says. I can tell the voice is being muffled by a handkerchief or something similar. I've done it a million times myself, ringing pizza shops and placing bogus orders or dialling at random and asking for people like Mr G. Raff or Iva Longin.

'Yeah, and?' I'm cautiously curious.

There's giggling.

'My friend reckons you're a bit of a spunk.'

I feel the muscles in my neck stiffen. I look around, almost expecting to see someone there ready to jump out and yell, 'Gotcha!'

'Who's your friend?' I say, because I can't think of anything else to ask.

More giggling. I'm trying to work out the voice but it's near impossible.

For a moment I wonder whether it might be . . .

Nah, Tracey wouldn't . . .

But then . . .

Nah . . .

'Hey, if this is a hoax call I'm going to . . .' I find myself saying.

'My friend reckons you're cute and wants to know why you're so shy around her. She wants to know if you like her. Do you?'

I consider a moment. This is critical. If this is a genuine call and I get the answer wrong I'm history. If it's a crank call and I give too much away I'm history, too. I decide to risk it.

'I reckon your friend should talk to me herself,' I say.

My stomach is doing cartwheels.

Just then Nonno pokes his head out into the hallway. 'Popes don't have the ghelfriends,' he smirks like he knows everything.

'Yeah, and old men like you don't have any respect for other people's privacy,' I say back, but with a laugh so that he doesn't go telling Mum that I'm being insolent. Insolent's a word I learned from Mum the last time Nonno dobbed on me for being rude to him.

'What?' The voice on the other end.

'Nothing,' I say. I take the plunge. 'This friend of yours, it isn't Tracey Reynolds, is it?'

'Could be.'

More giggles. Then, 'My friend sends you a smoochy kiss kissy,' the voice says. 'My friend says she loves boys with fast toys,' and hangs up.

I stand there for a few moments contemplating the receiver. It refuses to give me any clues to the caller so I set it back in its cradle.

Fast toys? The only fast toy I've got is the go-cart, and that's not even mine. It belongs to Bahmir's uncle.

I go back to the desk I have to share with some of Nonno's things but I can't settle. And besides, Nonno has filled in most of the blanks in my homework for me – with Italian words that have nothing to do with the classwork we've done in English on oral histories. I decide to pack it in for the night. I can't concentrate, anyway.

I lie there on my bed and think about flying away

from all this confusion. I think about the phone call. I think about Mum taking a basket of homebaked biscuits to the police station as a thanks to them for deciding not to take any further action against Nonno for taking the Porsche. And I think about what Dad might have been like to have a kick-to-kick with after school.

I lie there and think about so many things that I can't even decide if I feel like laughing or crying about what Nonno's done to my homework.

6

After school the next day, when I haven't managed to get any wiser about the strange phone call the night before, I explain the phone call to Nonno. I even tell Nonno my suspicion about the reference to the boys and their fast toys, and how I reckon the caller must have been referring to the go-carts that me, Dan and Bahmir race. But Nonno doesn't answer, doesn't offer any advice, mainly because he's fast asleep on the sofa.

I just needed to talk, and since I really don't want to tell Mum about my non-existent love-life, I figured telling Nonno would be the next best thing. Nonno's always been a good listener (when he's not asleep). He doesn't always understand what I'm on about, but he'll let me talk and talk. Sometimes that's all I need to do, is talk.

Earlier in the day I discovered there's no point trying to talk to Dan about the phone call. He's now convinced the little story about Don Nonno and the

Porsche will work real well with Tracey, sort of make me a mystery figure with a dark family background. Dan Declan watches too much TV.

It's moments like this I miss Dad. I like to think I would be able to tell Dad about my problems, especially with girls – or the lack of them.

Dad was great with girls. That's what all his mates reckoned, anyway. Everyone who knew Dad said he had a real funny streak, like he could make people laugh even when they tried hard not to. Girls liked that about him. That's how he and Mum first got together. Mum had been to see a soppy movie with her girlfriends and Dad saw her crying in the foyer afterwards. He went over and started acting the clown – just for something to do I guess, or maybe to cheer her up, and it all started from that.

Dad worked as a dogman for a small construction company. His job was to oversee the loading and unloading of the trucks that came on the construction sites. He was killed when a load of steel girders a crane was lifting off a flatbed semi-trailer gave way suddenly and he was pinned underneath. Dad was thirty-six years old.

I try not to think about the accident too much, but sometimes when I walk past a construction site, or I hear a whistle unexpectedly, I can't help it. I remember Mum coming into my room after school, after the police came and broke the news to her. I was just a kid, but I remember the sound of Mum's sobs as she cradled me in her arms and rocked back and forth.

That was one of the few times I've ever seen Nonno crying, the day Dad died. I saw him out of the corner of my eye in the doorway to the bedroom we share, sobbing into his hands. And I remember the look of agony on Nonno's face when he came over and hugged me so hard I thought he'd burst me.

That's probably why Mum and me are close. Because Dad's sudden death left a great big hole in the space where he used to be. Mum and me used to slot in alongside him and we've sort of huddled in close to fill that space as best we can. It would be good to have Dad around right now to bounce some ideas off. I bet Dad would know how to get Tracey Reynolds to notice me.

'*Sheeps.*'

I almost jump at the sound of Nonno's voice behind me. I've been walking round the lounge-room and didn't notice him stirring.

'Sheeps,' he says again.

I turn round and look at him.

'Yo, Nonno, you're awake,' I say and he looks at me as though I'm not conscious that this is the most obvious statement ever.

'In my village when boy like a ghel we take to hims father the sheeps,' Nonno beams.

I roll my tongue around and press it into one side of my mouth.

'You want impress dis ghel you need go see hims father and bring him . . .'

'Sheep?' I shake my head. Good one, Nonno, thanks. 'In Australia we don't bring sheep. Sometimes we take the girl flowers, or a bottle of wine for her old man, but sheep?'

Nonno stirs, shuffles his feet and licks his lips. When he yawns, his face looks as though it might be swallowed up by the big black abyss where his teeth should be.

No matter how many times I see Nonno minus his teeth I still get queasy. His dribble is worse when he doesn't have his teeth in.

'You want to pop your teeth in,' I tell him and watch as he reaches into the pocket of his waistcoat and puts his dentures back. He doesn't bother to go and rinse them out.

'You heard what I said?' I ask.

Nonno nods. 'Wot you tink, I sleep?'

I smile weakly. Nonno likes to think that he doesn't get any sleep. He tells anyone who'll listen about how he hasn't slept a wink in ten years.

'Well,' I begin, 'since I haven't got any sheep, I guess I'm out of luck with Tracey, eh.'

I smile again because I'm hoping he'll just nod and let me get away without any further explanation. I mean, talking to Nonno about my girl problems when he's asleep – or supposedly so, is one thing, but actually having to talk to him one on one about it . . .

I'd rather talk to Mum. Which is what I should do given that she is a girl as well, and she probably knows how girls think and all. But that would be just too awkward. I really don't know what to say to her.

I grin at Nonno. 'Do you know any good shepherds around these parts who might spare me a few sheep?' I ask.

Nonno clamps his chin in the palm of one hand, as though this is a serious question. To him I guess it is.

'Is not easy get sheeps,' he muses. 'No easy t'all.'

I leave Nonno contemplating sheep and go into the bedroom to get my things. Soon as Mum rocks up I have to go help Zia Rita sort out her stuff for the garage sale.

There's not much I want to take with me. Just hope the sale is well and truly over by the time I have to be at the go-cart track.

I'm packing my most recent CDs and thinking that maybe I should just front up to Tracey and tell her I know it was her who was behind the phone call, when Mum waltzes in.

She looks distracted. I can tell there's something on her mind even before she sits on the end of my bed, hands clasped on her lap.

'Paul,' she begins and I watch her eyes scan the room like maybe there's a camera hidden here to record what she's about to say.

'Paul,' she repeats and her voice is soft and low and a little breathless.

When she repeats my name *again*, I figure it's time to tell her that she's got that much right so far and would she like to move on to the next word.

'Paul, your dad has been dead five years now,' she says, looking over at Nonno's side of the room. This is where he keeps his odd collection of empty aftershave bottles, bottles Nonno has collected since way before even I was born. Every now and then Nonno will tell me about a certain bottle: who gave it to him, when, and how many of them still have a hint of their original smell, long after all the contents have gone. Nonno keeps the bottles on a packing crate he reckons he brought out from Italy with him. It says on the side of the crate: *Mildura Oranges – Fresh and Delicious. R. Trotter & Sons.*

'Paul, have I ever let you down?' Mum asks. It's one of those questions Lady Fang would ask: Mr Taranto, would you mind very much if you failed English this term? Mr Taranto, do you think your mother would be pleased to hear about your little escapade in science class today? Mr Taranto, is there a possibility you might actually write something coherent this period? Not real questions at all.

I stiffen.

'I don't think I ever have, have I, Paul?' Mum continues. I shake my head because otherwise she might stay on this one topic for the next few hours.

'And I never *would* let you down.' Mum's smoothing

over her jeans and I know for sure now she's all stressed out about what she has to say next. I figure I'll beat her to the punch.

'It's Nonno, right?' I pipe up in an effort to help her out. 'You can't take it any more and you've decided he needs more professional care.' I don't see what Mum does with her hands next because I'm walking round the bedroom shoving things into my bag to take with me to Zia Rita's.

'Maybe I can do more to help out with him,' I continue because I don't want to hear the rest of what I know Mum has come in here to tell me. 'Maybe I can stay home from school for a while and give you a break. I understand him, you know. Nonno's a bit wacky but he's okay with me . . .'

'Paul!'

I look at Mum. I know what she wants to say. She's had enough. She's tired. Zia Rita's right, after all. Nonno would be better off in a home.

I'd be better off with a bedroom to myself, I think suddenly. I can almost imagine spreading myself out in the bedroom without having to worry about where Nonno's dropped his walking-stick, or his teeth, or worry about knocking his precious aftershave bottles over . . .

'Paul!'

I look at Mum. She looks tired. And then something snaps inside me.

'Nonno doesn't really mean to be such a nuisance, Mum. You know that,' I say over the sudden thumping in my head.

'Paul, *what* are you talking about?'

I stop and look at Mum. She's staring right at me, her face total confusion.

'What?' I say helpfully.

Mum shakes her head slowly and hoods her eyes, passes a hand lightly over her forehead, then looks up at me again.

'Paul, would you mind very much if I went out to the movies?' she asks.

The movies.

She wants to go out to the movies.

'What about Nonno?' I ask.

'That's what I've come to ask you,' Mum goes on. 'I've asked Rita if Nonno can stay over with you tonight at her house while I go out to the movies.' Mum pauses. She's looking past me again.

'Do you *mind* very much if Nonno stays with you at Zia Rita's tonight? I know he'll probably slow you and Rita down a bit with getting things prepared...' Suddenly Mum stops and gets to her feet. 'Look, maybe it's not such a good idea.'

'You don't want to talk about Nonno?' I ask.

Mum shakes her head. 'No. Why would you think that, Paul?' She gives a hiccupped laugh. 'Paul, I just want to know if you'd be very disappointed in me if I went out to the movies tonight . . . with a man . . .'

I must have the word STUNNED painted right across my forehead, and my eyes must be bulging out of their sockets, because Mum drops her head and I hear a faint whimper of distress.

'Forget it, Paul,' she whispers. 'It was a silly idea. I'm sorry. You go to Zia Rita's and help out. You're right, Nonno will just be in the way.'

With a man. My mum?

But *her* man is dead. Dad's been gone five years already. Five long years. Mum's never gone out with anyone except Dad. I know because she told me herself. Dad was the one true and for ever love of her life.

A man! My mum?

Mum gets to her feet and crosses the short space between us in elegant strides. (She has a lot of style, my mum.) She gives me a kiss on the forehead. I can smell her. She's all talc and skin scrub lotion.

'Hurry up, Zia will be here soon,' she says.

I *am* stunned for a moment but finally I manage to ask, 'Who's the bloke? Anyone I know?' And then I have a wild thought and panic. For ages some of Mum's work friends have tried to fix Mum up with some desperados they'd dug out of some Italian community Search-For-Wife Program. Real losers with the personalities of a golf ball.

'Your friends haven't finally convinced you to match up with . . .' I start, but Mum shakes her head.

'Just as well,' I say and grin. I don't know how I'd feel about Mum seeing another man on those terms, although when I've talked to Dan about it, he reckons Mum's still young and one day she probably will find someone . . .

No, I'm lying. I know exactly how I'd feel about Mum seeing another man, on any terms. Shattered. Maybe that's why I'm shaking inside right now.

'Who you thinking of going to the movies with?' I ask finally.

I see Mum hesitate. She swallows.

'That cute young constable who came over to see us about the Porsche. He dropped by this afternoon to check if everything was okay with Nonno and . . . asked if I might like to catch a movie with him.'

Mum's voice is a million miles away. I'm in orbit somewhere around planet YOUMUSTBEKIDDING. I only just manage to hear Nonno ask from the doorway, 'Wot you tink, I need bring it my spare teeths?' before I crash and burn.

7

Zia Rita lives in a huge house left to her by her most recent husband, 'Uncle Freddie'. No one knows for sure why he left her the house. The husband before Uncle Freddie left Zia his vw Golf.

Sometimes I wish we were closer to Mum and Dad's relatives. But we're not. On Mum's side there's just Nonno's sister Marianna, but she lives in Detroit, and apart from the occasional letter or Christmas card, Nonno hasn't heard from her in ages. Nonna Romina left all her four brothers and three sisters behind in Italy when she followed Nonno out to Australia. I don't think they ever forgave her, even though Nonno sent her body back there for burial just as Nonna Romina had wanted. I asked Mum about that once, about how she felt about her own mum being buried so far away. Mum told me it was the right thing to do, to respect a person's last wishes. And besides, Mum said, Nonno knew that Nonna Romina had never felt truly at home here in Australia. I know Mum still hurts over not being able to visit Nonna's grave though, especially on Mothers' Day and All Saints Day.

Dad's family live in and around Mildura. They're all farming people. I've only met them a couple of times. Dad's only brother, Uncle Mick, is a top bloke. He's never married. He runs the family orchard with Dad's parents. They all came down for Dad's funeral, but not much after that.

There was a time about two years ago when whispers started that maybe Uncle Mick and Zia Rita should get together. He had property, she had property. They could have started a dynasty.

Mum laughed so loud at the idea that everyone said she blew Uncle Mick all the way back to Mildura.

So really, Zia Rita *is* my extended family. Oh, bliss and joy.

As expected, Zia Rita isn't rapt to have Nonno staying over. It's not in anything she says exactly, but I kind of got that impression when she asked me to make sure Nonno kept to the part of the house that faced the backyard.

For a second I think about suggesting to Zia Rita that maybe we should stick a 'For Sale' sign on Nonno's forehead and prop him up amongst the rest of the garage sale items and see what offers we get. I can see Nonno now, being prodded and poked by potential buyers, and then huffing as the bargain hunters try to nail me down to a rock-bottom price.

I can hear Nonno bark, 'Wot, you tink I is broke dat you want buy me too cheap?'

But I'm only joking. I'm still reeling over Mum going out with a cop. I can just hear Dan when he finds out about it. He'll tell everyone that of course my mum is going out with a policeman – isn't that the best way to keep abreast of any sniffing the cops might want to do into Don Nonno's affairs? Ha!

'You go out on dates much?' I ask Zia Rita, and help Nonno with his piano accordion. He's insisted on having it with him in the garage while Zia and me set up.

'That's a pretty personal question,' Zia Rita laughs, then adds, 'You thinking of fixing me up with someone?'

I shake my head. As if.

'I just thought, you know,' I begin cautiously. 'You know, Mum's just started . . . well, this is her first date in . . .' I can't remember the last time Mum even went out, I realise. Without me and Nonno tagging along, that is.

'Your mum is a very attractive woman,' Zia Rita tells me as I plonk Nonno in a chair and explain to him that he has to keep *out of the way*.

'When she was a teenager your mum had guys lining up to take her out. But you know what, she only ever went out with your dad.' Zia Rita shakes her head the way people do when they can't understand something. 'We've always been so different, your mum and me,' she adds.

Yeah? I think. But a cop? Why does Mum have to go out with a cop? Not that I have anything against the police. It's just . . . well, what will Dan and the other guys think of it all, Paul Taranto's mum going out on a date with a cop!

'You might have to get used to the idea of your mum seeing other men,' Zia Rita smiles, fussing over a framed poster of James Dean she's hoping to sell for twenty dollars. 'After all, Teresa is a young woman and it's unfair to expect her just to wilt away from neglect and deprivation behind closed doors.'

The words hit me in the middle of the forehead. I've never thought of my mum as wilting away. I have this image all of a sudden of my mum slowly turning browny-gold and stooped, and then doubling over until she starts to fall apart on our kitchen floor.

Young attractive mother of one found wilted in kitchen. Police suspect neglect and deprivation by only son as probable cause of death. That's how the banner headline of the daily newspaper would read.

'Tell me, Paul, this young constable your mum is going out with, is he good looking?'

I give Zia a quick glance. She's grinning at me.

'He's fat and short and has a receding hairline,' I answer. 'He has flat feet, big ears, a drooping moustache, and wears a suit that is two sizes too small for him.'

Zia Rita purrs. 'He sounds like a dish,' she sings. 'Lucky her.'

'Fish!' Nonno pipes up from his chair by the door. 'I not want fish. Get for me the dim sim . . . with sauce.'

I look at Nonno sitting there fiddling with his piano accordion and think of Mum. I can almost see the 'For Sale' sticker on Nonno's forehead. For five years now Mum's battled with Nonno on her own. She's nursed him, sat up with him all night when he's been agitated and confused, bathed and cleaned him, spoon fed him when he refuses to eat. She's even had to put up with him calling her by my dead nonna's name and asking her to come to bed. At least when Dad was alive they would take turns keeping Nonno amused and in line. But since Dad died Nonno's deteriorated even more.

I don't like the idea of Mum going out with anyone other than Dad, full stop. That's what I don't like, I tell myself finally.

But that's not fair on Mum. Zia Rita is right. Mum can't just 'wilt away' the way she has been doing these past five years.

It's like suddenly there are two voices inside my head talking to me at once. I suppose that deep down I know that the two voices have been there inside me for ages. My voice and Dad's. I've sort of always known that one day Mum would have to start getting her life back on track, that she is quite young, and that she can't go on just playing Mum to me and carer to Nonno. But . . .

I feel like one of those people from some B-grade

horror flick who are driven crazy by the voices at war in their heads.

'Maybe I should buy Mum a dog,' I say suddenly, and the moment the words are out I know I sound like a dork.

Zia Rita is lifting a carton of books she wants to parcel up into bundles of three and sell for five dollars a bunch. She laughs out loud.

'A *dog*?' she splutters and drops the carton at my feet. 'That's a good one, Paul.'

'There's nothing wrong with dogs,' I say. 'They're good companions.'

'I had dog hwuen I wos boy,' Nonno offers. He's frowning in my direction. I wonder if he's understood what's going on. 'Him not taste too good.'

I close my eyes real tight and shake my head. I can hear Zia Rita cackling near by. When I open my eyes again Nonno is looking sad, his hands motionless over the keys of the piano accordion.

'You see how they laugh at an old man,' he says softly. 'You gets old and evrihuan tinks they can laugh at you.'

I feel a twinge of something in my chest. It could be indigestion because Zia insisted we have curried eggs and saffron rice for dinner, but somehow I don't think it is and that worries me even more.

'Zia's not laughing at you, Nonno,' I say as gently as I can. 'She just doesn't get it, you know.'

And she doesn't. Not about Nonno, and not about Mum and me, either. I was going to ask her for advice about Tracey but I don't think I will now. She might just tell me to do something radical like tell Tracey exactly how I'm feeling.

Or worse, she might tell me to get a *life*.

'Play something up-beat, Dad,' Zia Rita tells Nonno. She's emptying books onto the floor and lengths of ribbon lie scattered ready for bundling the books into parcels. 'Play one of those . . .' Zia fumbles for the term a moment. 'Mazurkas . . . Play one of those. Or a Tarantella. They're always fun. Go on. Like you did when Teresa and I were kids. Remember?'

I want to tell Zia that Nonno only remembers sporadically. Sometimes he can remember things from when he was a kid more than seventy years ago, and other times he can't even remember what he's had for dinner that night.

Zia is dancing in the silence, her arms out over her head, her head to one side.

It doesn't take long for Nonno to start playing, and when he does Zia Rita grabs me by both hands and we whirl around her garage the way we did at family get-togethers before Dad died. I do my best not to topple over as Zia pulls me in every direction at once, her mouth open like those clowns at Luna Park you drop ping-pong balls into. I see Nonno hunched over his piano accordion. His head is rocking from side to side and his eyes are closed. There is a grin on his face and his right foot is tapping time.

'Gee, I miss this stuff!' Zia cries as we lock arms and twirl and stomp our feet.

So do I. I miss it, too. I miss the music and the laughter, and I miss Dad.

I miss the old Nonno, too. The Nonno before he started drifting away. The Nonno who used to never forget my name, or that Mum's name is Teresa and not Romina.

I miss all this, and Mum and Dad laughing at each other's sick jokes, and this and Mum and Dad swinging me between them as they dance. This and Mum and Dad cradling me as I fall asleep amongst all the noise and music and voices of their friends crowded into our one-car garage at Christmas or Easter, or my birthday . . .

But I say nothing because there's a great big lump sitting right there in my throat and if I even try to speak it will choke me.

Nonno's music stops after a while and I'm looking at Zia. She's all flushed and red in the face. Her always-so-neat hair is all messed up, and she's huffing and puffing trying to catch her breath.

She's so picture perfect in all her details, my zia. My mum can't afford to be. She's always on the run, from home to work and back again. It's a constant struggle for her to even find time to sit with me long enough to realise I'm still reading the same book in Term 4 as I was back in Term 1.

If Mum's not chasing me about homework she's chasing Nonno, or bringing him home again when he wanders off. He's started doing that more often now. He'll quietly wander out the back door and down the street. He says he needs to get the goats back to the barn. If Mum's not apologising to the neighbours because I've sent a cricket ball soaring through their back window, she's explaining to them why they shouldn't take Nonno's yelling at them to move out seriously.

Zia Rita went to Fiji for two weeks over the Easter break this year. Mum spent three days rushing in and out of St Vincents Hospital between shifts at work because Nonno tripped over his walking-stick on Good Friday and gave himself concussion.

All this is going through my mind as Zia Rita stands there grinning at me, so I dare myself to say what I'm thinking. 'It's about time you gave Mum a rest and took care of Nonno for a while.' I speak slowly so that Zia can't help but hear every word.

'I mean,' I continue, 'I mean, Mum and me, we love Nonno and all. We love him very much. It's just time for Mum to have a break from him, and for you and Nonno to get to know each other again.'

It's time for you to stop pretending like nothing's changed since Dad died and Nonno has started acting like he's lost the script to the play the rest of us seem to be caught up in so he makes it up as he goes. It's time for you to stop being so careless about your own dad and start taking some responsibility for him.

That's what I would say if the words would come out, but they don't, so all I add when Zia gives me a stare to melt concrete is, 'Mum needs to get a life.' She *is* going out tonight with a cop, after all. I mean, how desperate is that!

If Nonno hears what I've said he doesn't make any sign of it. He just starts playing away on his accordion, his head rocking back and forth, his foot tapping time.

'You and Nonno *are* her life, Paul,' Zia says through a smile she's ripped right out of one of those bizarre magazine ads for haemorrhoid creams. She's got her hands on her hips and she's breathing through her nose. I can see her nostrils flaring like bellows.

'I thought you and Nonno were mates,' she adds and nods in Nonno's direction.

Nonno and me are better than mates, we're blood brothers. Nonno told me that years ago. He said that in Monte Sereno old people were revered. The old people hold all the folklore and traditions and stories and myths of the village in their minds for the next generation. Nothing is written down, everything depends on the old people telling their stories.

Without the stories, Nonno says, the village would crumble and die. It would be without a soul.

I think of a village where the people roam lost and without purpose. I look at Zia Rita.

'Has your mother put you up to this, Paul?' Zia asks. 'Hasn't she got the courage to ask me herself to take Nonno off her hands? Does she want me to stick a "For Sale" sign on his forehead maybe and off-load him for her!' Zia Rita's voice is brittle, like it's going to snap.

I stare at her and then at Nonno. The Don. Yeah, that'd be about right, Zia. Get rid of the old bloke like he's some out-of-fashion jacket or wall hanging! Problem is, *I* don't *want* to sell him.

'Mum doesn't want Nonno "off her hands", Zia,' I reply instead with anger. Suddenly, dancing away here in her huge garage, in the middle of her huge property, with Nonno there on the chair banging away at his piano accordion, I can't help but be totally annoyed at Zia for the way she's always dismissed Nonno and Mum.

I know my mum would go ballistic if she heard what I'd said to my zia. Mum would never even think of asking Zia Rita to take Nonno for a few days so that she could have a break. Never.

It's only then, when Zia Rita opens her mouth to tell me I have no right to say what I've said and her voice booms under the aluminium roof, that I realise Nonno has stopped playing.

8

Even in Zia's house, with its five bedrooms and three toilets, a gigantic billiards room and monster kitchen, I still had to share a room with Nonno last night. Zia was afraid that being in a strange environment might unsettle Nonno and he might wake suddenly and then what?

And then it would be just like any other night when he's woken suddenly and started talking to Nonna Romina, or to Dad, or sometimes even to people I've never heard of. I just lie in bed and listen and watch him from the shadows for that hour or so it takes him to settle again.

It wasn't Nonno who kept me up most of last night, though. My mind kept me awake, replaying images of me telling Zia Rita it was time she took over from her sister a bit and looked after their dad. I mean, I've never thought about it much, how Zia's always managed to avoid doing her share. I've always figured that because Nonno has chosen to live with Mum and me that that's the way it has to be . . . for ever. Guess I'm starting to figure differently.

The garage sale is going pretty well this morning. At the rate things are moving Zia won't have anything left to sell come lunchtime. Then I can get to the go-cart track. The sooner the better, I reckon. The first browsers arrived while we were still having breakfast. Despite saying she wouldn't open until after breakfast, Zia rushed out and bargained the sale of an old pot-bellied stove, two tiffany lamps and a terracotta vase filled with artificial iris.

I haven't heard from Mum yet. Not that I expected to, I guess. Wonder how her date went. I reckon she's probably spent the entire time cruising the backblocks of the docks area in a divvy van tailing suspicious-looking groups of teenagers. Or maybe he took Mum on an exciting tour of the local police station, pointing out the cells to her and telling her how he takes finger-prints and showing her his cuffs and baton.

Either way I'm glad the date is over. And I don't want to know any details. It's enough that I have to know my mum went out on a date at all.

'How much for the books?'

I'm staring at Nonno sitting in the same spot where he was last night – minus the 'For Sale' sign. I look at the mess he's making with the pistachio shells and don't recognise the voice at first.

'The paperbacks are five dollars a bundle and the hardcovers are five dollars each, or best offer,' I say with authority. I want to move all this junk as quickly as possible.

And that's when I look up and see Lady Fang standing an arm's length away, studying two bundles of paperbacks. She has her eyes narrowed and is juggling the bundles in her hands as though she's weighing them.

'I'll take both for seven dollars,' she says stiffly. 'Not a dollar more.'

And that's when she recognises me. I know because her face drops. I know what she's thinking: she's thinking it's Saturday. Do I have to see you on Saturdays too, Mr Taranto?

She doesn't say that, though. Instead she hugs the bundles and fumbles for her purse, fishes out seven dollars and holds it out to me.

'You live around here, Miss Wildermere?' I ask, but I don't take her money.

When Lady Fang doesn't answer I call out to ask my zia if the price offered for the bundles suits her, and add that this is my homeroom and English teacher, so that the other browsers in the garage all hear.

'I'm just helping out my aunty,' I offer and take the money. 'This huge house is a family heirloom,' I add. 'We've decided to free up space by getting rid of junk we don't need any more, so's we can have more room for the new furniture and stuff that's coming out from Italy soon.'

Lady Fang clears her throat and licks her lips. I can see that she's impressed with the garden and the look of the house. I would be, too. Zia has a gardener come out once a week to do the lawns and shrubs and stuff, and the house itself is a beautiful red brick with black brick offset.

'I'd hardly call selling books of poems by Tennyson and Byron and Dickinson, getting rid of *junk*, Mr Taranto,' she says, hugging the bundles to her chest.

I smile. This is fun. Not as good as go-carting, but this part is way cool.

'The library inside is crammed with books by those people, Miss,' I grin. 'These are just spare copies of cheap reprints that my aunt no longer has space for.'

Lady Fang sniffs. I was the last person on earth she expected to run into this morning, I bet.

'I thought you lived on the other side of town, Miss Wildermere?' I know for a fact that she lives a good half-hour's drive away.

'I'm in the area,' Lady Fang begins.

'Do you like garage sales then, Miss?' I ask. 'You can get some really cheap bargains I bet, eh, especially on a teacher's wage and all.' I smile because I don't want another detention when we get back to school. I'm just making conversation with a customer, after all.

'*Inexpensive*, Mr Taranto,' Lady Fang hisses.

Inexpensive. Cheap. It doesn't matter. Lady Fang is a garage sale junkie I've decided, and she knows I think that, because she starts to explain herself and then decides she has to be somewhere else. Another garage sale maybe.

'Miss Wildermere.'

I hear Mum's voice before I see her. She's standing in the shadow of the overhanging elm tree just outside the garage. Lady Fang has fair run into her on her way out.

'Fancy you being here,' Mum adds. 'I hope my sister hasn't had to call you in to get Paul under control!' Mum gives a cackled laugh. A snort really, but Lady Fang isn't in the mood for jokes and after a quick hello takes off at speed down the driveway.

'Strange lady,' Mum says with a sly grin and steps over a rolled-up fake Persian rug to get to me. She plants a kiss on my forehead.

A kid looking through Zia's CD cast-offs gives me a snigger. I give him the finger.

'Aren't you supposed to be at work?' I ask and immediately wish I'd said hello first because Mum's face drops slightly.

'Can't a mother drop by on her way to work to say hi to her son?' she asks, but I know it's not a question at all. 'How's Nonno?'

Mum can see for herself that Nonno is fine. He hasn't noticed her yet. He's busy making a face on the floor using discarded nutshells.

'Teresa, how was The Great Date?'

Zia Rita is at my elbow. She's carrying a knot of plastic bags. Her question was a question, but it had the sound of a challenge in it. I know, because I've asked questions like that myself: so, you think you can take me on, do you? Did you like dobbing me in, did you? You haven't got a boyfriend, have you, Mum?

Mum is about to answer Zia's question but I guess Zia doesn't have time for the answer because she suddenly gets really interested in the kid going through her CD collection.

'Is anything wrong, Paul?' Mum asks.

I shrug. What can I tell her? That I've put the hard word on Zia about Nonno? That we've both thought about putting a 'For Sale' sign on Nonno's forehead and passing him off to some unsuspecting buyer? Don't think so.

'So, did he show you his pistol?' I ask instead.

'What?'

Stupid!

'Who?'

Stupid!

'Paul, are you being stupid?'

'How was last night?' I whisper. It's like I don't want anyone else to hear.

Mum shrugs. 'Okay.'

That's it? Okay. What does 'okay' mean?

Mum steps past me to Nonno and gives him a kiss

71

on the cheek. Nonno smiles when he realises who it is.

'You're out of jail!' he grins in Italian.

Mum sighs slowly. I see her shoulders go up and down as Nonno hugs her and slaps her gently on the back.

'You mama she out of the jail,' he smiles and winks at me, and I sort of cringe because the two people standing with Zia Rita looking at her framed poster of James Dean are smirking.

'The judge said he'd go lenient on her this time, Nonno,' I say through a huge mock sigh. 'But she knows that the next time she holds up a bank to pay for my education it'll be a long stretch . . . again!'

The two people near Zia look suitably startled. The woman is trying hard to look like she hasn't been eavesdropping, while the man is blinking into space.

Mum rounds on me with one of her cold stares.

'It's good to have you home, Mum,' I grin.

By the time Zia has negotiated the sale of James Dean, Mum has explained to me about how she'll come by on her way home from work and collect me and Nonno. And I've arranged for her to agree to pizza for dinner.

'Anything you want to talk about?' Zia Rita asks Mum sternly when she comes across and drops the ten dollars in coins from the James Dean sale into the money tin with a loud clatter.

Mum screws up her mouth and shakes her head.

'I don't think it's fair that you use Paul to sound me out like this, Teresa,' Zia begins in a whisper so's Nonno won't hear. 'I mean, if you want to look seriously at a home for Dad, then by all means let's discuss the options. I've still got all the brochures and stuff on those places I sussed out last year. But *pleeese*, don't patronise me by trying to have me agree to taking Dad in, only to have *me* then be the one to do the deed.'

'Sorry?'

Mum is looking a lot like she did when the police called to ask about the Porsche. I figure it's time to bail out, but how?

'Don't "sorry" me, Sis,' Zia says with more than a little huff in her tone. 'I knew that sooner or later Dad would become too much of a burden for you. I mean, *I'm* the one who told you he should have been admitted ages ago.' Zia does a kind of rolling half-twist with her head and throws both hands up, palms out to Mum. '*You're* the one who wanted to play the martyr with him.'

'Paul?' Mum is frowning. 'What on earth have you been saying to Rita?'

Good one!

I spot a man going through some of Zia's mismatched cutlery and wine glasses and shoot across to help him out.

'*Paul?*'

I don't answer. It's the best option really. Silence

and a goofy smile that sort of says, why is it that adults always misunderstand everything I tell them?

Behind me I hear Mum draw a breath, then tell her sister that she's going to be late for work and would she mind keeping her daydreams to herself.

'Ciao, Papa,' Mum calls to Nonno and he lifts a hand in slow recognition. 'Don't you cause any revolutions while I'm at work, okay?'

I toss a price off the top of my head at the man looking at the cutlery and look towards Nonno. He's sitting up, back straight. Well, straight for a man in his seventies, anyway.

'You girls argue too much,' he says in Italian, then adds in English, 'I not be a dog wot dies in a strange kennel.'

'That's why you should stay at Teresa's,' Zia Rita replies flatly. 'My house is just too strange for someone your age.'

I sell two lots of quality cutlery to the man who is admiring them at a low price not even he could have imagined. Then I throw in a set of brandy tumblers for nothing. My zia can afford it, I decide.

'We don't drink,' I smile at the astonished man and hand him his purchases. He saunters off, grinning, and I crumple the five dollar note in my hand. I think he appreciates my generosity because as he's leaving he calls out to Zia that I'm a top salesman and nods to the few others still browsing that I'm their man.

I grin sheepishly at my zia who is standing, hands on hips, smiling at nothing in particular.

Two hours later and we're through. Zia hands me twenty dollars for my efforts and I help pack away what's left of the odds and ends. I elbow Nonno back into the house where Zia has had open sandwiches and pumpkin soup delivered from the gourmet deli down the street. I hoe into lunch with more appetite than I thought I had.

'Nonno needs to get a few hours sleep,' I tell Zia when we've finished, and before she can complain about putting him on the couch, I have Nonno's shoes and waistcoat off and lean his walking-stick in one corner. Then I tear out the back door, calling out that I'll be back in a few hours.

'What . . . I . . . with . . . when . . . wakes . . . ?' Zia's question follows me down the sweeping driveway.

'Talk to him!' I call back. Zia doesn't know it as well as Mum and I do, but Nonno loves to talk. Not about anything in particular. You just sort of let him go and do your best to stay with him.

She's going to have an interesting afternoon, my zia Rita, and she deserves to, especially if she's silly enough to bring up the topic of old people's homes.

I'm laughing, and cough up pumpkin soup through my nostrils. Good thing Dan isn't around to see it. Or worse still, gorgeous and stylish Tracey, who'd never blow pumpkin soup out through *her* nose.

9

Nonno took me to the Melbourne Formula 1 Grand Prix the year after Dad died. Nonno was still pretty clear-headed then. He had his moments of course, like forgetting which tram we had to catch home, but back then his lapses were just occasional. You could almost convince yourself that he was playing a trick, and that maybe it was just a little test he was putting you through.

That was when I decided I wanted to be a Formula 1 race driver. And not just any driver, but a World Champion Formula 1 driver for an Australian team. When I told Nonno about my ambition he smiled and told me *anything* was possible. When I told Mum she smiled and asked whether I might consider a less life-threatening career, like computer science maybe. That was about four years ago now and I've never told Mum again because she's got enough to worry about already.

I'd love to take Nonno to the go-cart track with me

one day but I can't be sure how he'd react to all the noise and the smell, and the sight of me tearing around in those two-stroke carts like a madman.

If I'm really honest, one of the major reasons I don't take Nonno with me is that he'll probably do something to totally embarrass me. Like throw pistachio shells at the other competitors as they file past under the viewing platform, and tell them that I'm the best Formula 1 driver in the world. Or call out for his dead wife, my nonna Romina, to shut the door against all the noise because it's giving him a headache.

Or start crying because he forgets where he is and can't recognise anyone else on the viewing platform.

I'm thinking all this as I enter the track when Dan spots me and charges my way.

'Thought you were doing a no-show,' he says.

'Yeah, hi to you, too,' I reply and keep walking. Then I add, 'The garage sale went well this morning. Thanks for asking.'

'You've only got a few minutes to do a couple of warm-up laps,' Dan tells me and we break into a jog.

I'm scanning the joint looking for any signs of Tracey. I *had* heard Dan right, hadn't I? He did say Tracey was coming with Magda to watch us race? Dan must read my mind because he pulls me up short and twists my head so that I'm looking towards the kiosk.

'She got here with Magda about a half hour ago,' he tells me.

'Who?' I try to sound as though I have no idea what Dan is on about.

'Yeah, right, Taranto, *who*?' Dan grins and shoves me in the middle of the back so that I stagger forward and into the pit area where Bahmir is waiting.

'Romeo has arrived,' Dan announces.

Bahmir, who is hunched over adjusting his shoes, looks up and grins.

Bahmir is a cool kid. He has a gold stud in his left nostril and a scar he got from a minibike crash when he was in Year 6 running across the top of his lip like some hairline moustache. Bahmir is a whiz at school. He tops the maths and the science classes every year. If it wasn't for the stud and the scar you'd think he was a nerd.

Sometimes I wonder about getting a nose stud. Then I think how hard it would be to try and survive out on the streets once my mum got a look at it.

'So, I hear you got a hot phone call the other night,' Bahmir grins in my direction. 'Magda couldn't *resist* telling me.'

Bahmir and Dan laugh. I give them two fingers, one from each hand, and go collect my racing gloves.

Because Bahmir, Dan and me are regulars at the track we've supplied our own gear and keep it on site. The fact that Bahmir's uncle, Mr Ganhisham, runs the place helps too, I guess.

'Don't worry, Taranto.' It's Dan at my shoulder.

'Magda has already broken the ice for you with Tracey.'

There are worms in my stomach and they have nothing to do with being anxious about racing.

'Meaning what exactly, do you reckon?' I ask as off-handedly as I can.

Bahmir winks at me and tosses me my helmet. I catch it with one hand and try not to drop my gaze from his.

'Meaning that Tracey Reynolds knows that you have the hots for her,' Dan cuts in. 'Meaning Tracey Reynolds is here to see what you're made of, *mate*.' Dan says the word mate like he's biting it in two.

'Flesh and bone,' I say back because it's all I can think of (and I heard *that* once on a TV show, too, and I know I have to say something). 'Flesh and bone.'

Bahmir and Dan make as though they want to chuck and they turn on their heels, laughing. 'Boner more like it, Taranto, and a winny one at that,' Dan tosses over his shoulder. 'Hey, Taranto,' he adds, 'you broken any more sprockets lately?'

By the time I get out onto the pit proper I'm sweating. I can't even look up at the viewing platform. I know Tracey is there. I know she's looking at me and sizing me up, deciding just how much of a dork or otherwise I am.

I don't want to think about it.

Formula 1 drivers have to put any personal

thoughts and problems aside when they climb into their machines, and that's exactly what I have to do now. Drivers who take their personal lives and concerns into the cars with them run the risk of crashing out or worse. Formula 1 driving is all about concentration, about being focused, about . . .

'You actually going to climb into your cart or what?' Mr Ganhisham, Bahmir's uncle, is standing beside me.

'It's easier to drive the cart when you're sitting in the driver's seat,' Mr Ganhisham says, and points at the cart in front of me. I'm standing almost in the driver's seat and hadn't even realised it.

Black mark one against my name and reputation, I decide, as I cringe down into the seat and adjust my seat belt. I hope Tracey just thinks I always stand beside my cart and meditate before the warm-up laps.

The go-cart is light and fast, and pretty soon I've put Tracey Reynolds out of my mind. I have to because we're racing against top-notch drivers from across town, from one of the posh suburbs. They have their *own* carts and all. They have family here to watch them and cheer them on. Dan, Bahmir and I only have Magda, Tracey and a few hangers-on.

Bahmir's uncle arranges these comps every so often. Sometimes we even get to race on other tracks and he loads up the carts and takes us all to the venues. Mr Ganhisham used to be a jockey but he reckons horses are too expensive to maintain and that's why he got into go-carts. There's a logic there somewhere, I guess.

Mum isn't rapt in the idea of me racing the carts, but she figures they're a whole lot safer than some of the other stuff I could be doing. So she lets me race. But she's made me promise never to take stupid risks.

She doesn't need to worry but, because I'm a good driver.

I'm not bragging when I say I'm the best driver on our team, but I am . . . the best driver, that is. Dan reckons I'm reckless. Bahmir reckons I've got a death wish. I just reckon if you want to win a race you have to be in front at the end.

And that's where I am, out front, with two laps to go. Dan is in my slipstream, and behind him one of the opponent drivers is doing his best to tailgate him. I know because every now and then I catch a quick glimpse over my shoulder. I can almost hear the sweat pouring off Dan's forehead. I bet his eyes are bulging against his goggles and if he grips the steering wheel any tighter it's going to be permanently attached to his palms.

GO . . .
BAH . . . MIRRRR . . .
ON YA DANN . . .
STAY . . .
OUT . . .
FRONT . . .

TA...RAN...TOOOOOO...

The cheers are like spits of rain in your face as you race past the viewing stand and into the right-hand turn at the end of the straight. You feel as though you're right out there in a Formula 1 when you catch a whiff of cheering.

I gun the engine and hear the wheels screech, the rubber laying thick on the asphalt.

GO...

DON PAUL...

GOOO...

The voice hits me square between the eyes. A beautiful, sexy voice, even when it's diced up by the slipstream and the whine of the carts' engines.

Tracey Reynolds calling my name, urging me on, urging me to stay out in front!

I nearly lose it on the next corner.

Hearing your name called out by the sexiest girl alive can have that effect on a guy. But somehow I manage to correct the slide and ease the cart back into a straight line, narrowly missing Dan who had time to come up on my left.

That's all I can hear, Tracey Reynolds calling my name. The engine, the wind, and the squeal of the rubber on the track as I take a corner tightly.

The last lap is the hardest. I have to will myself to ease up enough so's not to run the engine too hard and risk it conking out on me. I want to be way out in front where I can be on my own, where Tracey can get a really good look at my driving skills without the distraction of there being other carts around to spoil the view.

The finish line sneaks up on me and I know as I cross it that I've won by a huge margin. My legs and hands are aching, my eyes are filling with sweat that's dripping down the inside of my helmet, and my throat is parched. Twenty-three laps I've raced but I feel like I could do another hundred if Tracey stays there on the viewing platform and urges me on!

'Boy, you got a fire up your bum or what?' Mr Ganhisham says to me as I climb out of the cart and take high-fives from Dan and Bahmir.

'Nah,' says Dan through a laugh, 'just a little extra heat under the bonnet. Ain't that right, Taranto?'

For the first time since Tracey became a fixture in my mind I smile at Dan and don't bother wise-cracking him back. This feeling inside is just too good for that sort of stuff. Too good.

Up on the viewing platform I see Tracey Reynolds. She's smiling in my direction. I smile back and punch the air like I've just won a Grand Prix before my home crowd.

Right then, I'm sort of grateful I didn't bring Nonno along.

10

Don Paul Taranto, hero. Racing hero. Go-cart legend and all-round heart throb.

Yes!

It's late afternoon and my team has won three of the four races. I won two of the three, so I'm flying high.

Winning is terrific, but I'm flying high too because Tracey has just told Magda to tell me that Tracey would like me to buy her a hot dog and Coke. In celebration of my great driving.

And do you think Don Paul would mind if I asked him to let me be privileged enough to actually go for a spin in his 1957 Corvette Roadster, or maybe in his Bell Jetranger helicopter? I mean, I know there are just sooo *many other girls lining up for the chance to be seen with him, but do you reckon he . . .*

I crack it for a grin but can't look directly at Magda when I nod to tell her it's okay and that I'd love to buy

Tracey a hot dog. Could be the sun in my eyes. Or maybe the fact that my stomach is twisted in knots.

Lucky for me my zia was generous with her tip this morning because usually I'm sponging off Dan for a few dollars to buy stuff. Not that Mum is cheap. She's not. Mum gives me so much a week, but it's just that lately the weeks have either shrunk or grown because I never have enough to see out more than about two days – three tops! I've made a deal with Mum to get a part-time job somewhere. Just for after school Fridays and Saturdays. Macca's sounds good, but the waiting list at the local is heaps long.

'That was some pretty fancy driving, Paul.' Tracey Reynolds's first words directly to me. She's holding the hot dog I've bought her and is looking sideways at me.

'Yeah,' I sort of murmur back when what I really want to say is, 'Can I have a kiss, then?'

Dan is being an axehead because he's standing just behind Tracey and making pouting faces in my direction. But he can make all the faces he wants because I'm not about to ruin my chances by being an imbecile and laughing out loud.

Girls like Tracey, cool chicks with cool attitude, hate imbeciles. I know, because Mum let it slip that when she first met Dad's best mate she thought he was an imbecile. Why? Because all he ever did was grin stupidly and laugh at nothing in particular.

'My old boyfriend in Queensland, Matt, he used to

race slot cars,' Tracey goes on. 'But after watching you guys burn round the track the way you did, slot cars are tame as.'

Tracey eats slowly so I find myself doing likewise. I mean, I don't want to come across as a hog by wolfing my hot dog down the way I usually would. It's hard though, because Tracey takes small bites and seems to chew each mouthful about a hundred times before she swallows. She doesn't even take a swig from her Coke until her mouth's empty.

'Hey,' Tracey smiles, 'is it true your grandfather nicked a Porsche and the cops were too scared to charge him, so they let him go?' She's looking at me and her mouth is slightly open so that I can just see the perfect line of her straight teeth.

'Sort of, I guess,' I shrug, because I don't actually want to confirm or deny the story. My nonno and the Porsche are becoming a bit legendary around the place. I don't even bother explaining that the Porsche in question was a scale model – a very good scale model, actually. Kids at school reckon my nonno must be way cool. Who am I to argue?

'That's just awesome,' Tracey whispers, and moves her head so her hair bobs around in the breeze. 'Must be cool having a grandfather who's so powerful and stuff. Bahmir reckons your grandfather is known as The Don. Is that true?'

I nod vaguely. 'Yeah,' I say through clenched teeth.

Tracey smiles. 'Bahmir reckons that you're known as Don Paul in your family.'

Don Paul?

I'm about to explain to Tracey that the only reason Dan and Bahmir nicknamed my nonno The Don after the Porsche incident is that they watch too many American gangster shows on cable TV. And because they like to stir me up.

Before I can say anything though, Tracey adds, 'Do you guys have big family meetings and stuff? You know, like in the movies, with blokes that look like gorillas out the front and back of the house, and long black limos in the driveway?' Tracey is looking directly at me. She has this glint in her beautiful eyes. I have to look away.

'We have get-togethers,' I say, but don't bother adding that the get-togethers usually only involve Mum, Nonno, me and Zia Rita when she decides to front. Just us four and Mum's taralli biscuits, marinated squid, and maybe a glass of marsala wine. I don't mention that the only things outside our front or back doors are concrete and grass, neither of which is very threatening.

Not like Nonno can be sometimes, when the family spirit becomes too much for him and he starts to cry and babble, and asks me to make sure the doors are bolted because the enemy might be near by. He never says who the enemy is, but Mum says Nonno sometimes probably confuses the noises he hears with the sounds of war from when he was about my age back in Italy.

Thinking about this now I'm *extra* glad I didn't bring Nonno along.

It's strange how just sitting here beside Tracey Reynolds can make me feel like I've got sunburn. I've got a raging pulse of heat all down the side of my body that's closest to her, and I reckon I might be about to melt where our knees are touching.

Promising young driving ace loses leg to mysterious melting disease. Rest of body not good either. Cause unknown, although speculation now centres on mystery girl with char marks along left leg.

'The phone call the other night,' Tracey finally cuts into my thoughts. 'That was Magda's idea. She's a real scream sometimes.' She's smirking like it's such a joke. 'Hope you didn't mind too much.'

'Nah,' I say too quickly. 'No . . . girls always ring . . .'

Tracey narrows her eyes.

Dork! I'm a dork!

'I mean . . .' I try, but Tracey just smiles.

'You got anything you need to be doing after this?' Tracey asks suddenly.

I've got my can up to my lips and splash Coke up my nostrils.

'Nah . . . I mean, no,' I manage to get out, pinching the end of my nose and doing my best to lick the Coke from my face before Tracey notices.

'Cool,' she smiles and shuffles over a little bit closer to me. 'I've invited Magda and Bahmir to my place after this. You want to come along?'

Tracey has finished her hot dog and is licking the tiniest drop of tomato sauce from the corner of her mouth. Even doing this she looks stunning, with her hazel eyes and her oval face.

'I like you . . . Don Paul, you're different,' she grins and gives me a wink. Not one of Dan's weirdo-twisted winks, but a slow wink that makes my skin tingle.

I'm different!

Tracey Reynolds reckons I'm different. From what or who exactly I don't know and I don't care. Tracey has noticed me enough to notice that much about me, and that's heaps.

And she's invited me to her place.

Dan wanders over and stands grinning at us.

Tracey is next to me. I want to take her hand but I don't want to push it, so I just let my arms drop by my sides. I'm hoping she'll take my hand instead.

'So, Hot Shot, how's it going?' Dan asks and winks at me.

I grin.

'You don't mind if I take Don Paul away from you for a while, do you Danny?' Tracey asks. I see Dan frown. No one ever calls him Danny. He hates being called Danny. Even with the teachers, only Lady Fang calls him Danny.

I can see Dan is annoyed. He's looking right at me.

'The name's *Dan*,' Dan says harshly.

Tracey nods. 'Dan,' she whispers, then adds, 'You two guys haven't got anything planned for the rest of the day, have you? Together, I mean.'

Dan grins. He shakes his head. I know he doesn't really like Tracey, but what am I supposed to do?

I don't say anything. Neither does Tracey. It's Dan who saves the moment.

'I'm not his keeper,' he says with a shrug. Then to me: 'I'll be down at Rocco's checking out the new games if you need to come looking for me.'

And with that, Dan gives me a final wink and turns away. After a few steps he stops and calls over his shoulder, 'That was some really great driving out there, mate. Don't take your foot off the accelerator now, okay?'

I'm not sure what Dan means exactly, but I think he's wishing me good luck.

Paul Taranto, you're legend material for absolute sure.

11

Tracey Reynolds's house is a mansion. There are four toilets, including one in the garage. Not even Zia Rita has a toilet in her garage.

Nonno would love this. The lawn out back is so soft and green. It looks like carpet. Nonno could play a mean game of bocce on this, no worries.

I can't believe I'm actually playing pool with Bahmir on a full-size table in the middle of an enormous room that overlooks a kidney-shaped pool. Dan would be rapt to have a game on a table like this – one that doesn't have a dozen repair patches sewn into the felt.

'Anyone for a drink?' Tracey calls from behind the bar where a mirror at her back reflects me standing with the cue stick in hand, gawking at the surrounds.

'Yeah, thanks,' I go and saunter over to Tracey while Bahmir lines up his shot. 'Your folks must be loaded,' I say before I can bite my tongue.

But Tracey doesn't flinch. I guess she must be used to people stating the obvious when they first see the house.

There are four large glasses lined up on the bar and Tracey pours a measure of whisky into each.

I don't drink. Well, not apart from the table wine Mum lets me have with dinner occasionally. Or the nip of Nonno's grappa I've had once or twice when he's offered his hipflask to me in our bedroom. Or the stubby or two Dan has managed to get for us after a particularly good Carlton win. But I don't admit to it. Not with Tracey pouring the drinks.

'Whisky,' I say instead. 'You always go straight for the hard stuff?' I add this with a grin.

Tracey smirks. 'It's a heart starter,' she answers slowly. 'Dad keeps the really good stuff under lock and key. Says it's for his "valued friends". This'll have to do. Here.'

Tracey holds a glass out to me and smiles. She lifts her own glass to her lips and sips from it, her eyes on me.

I swallow and swing back, too quickly. The whisky sloshes in my mouth and I close my eyes for the big gulp. Dan would know how to get this down the right way.

I feel it coming but I can't stop. A major cough and a huge splutter explode from my mouth. I double over and the glass rocks in my hand, whisky splashing the carpet.

Tracey's laugh is just like the sound iced water makes when you pour it into a long glass on a sweltering day.

'You're not supposed to scull it, silly,' Tracey says and puts an arm around my shoulder.

There's an inferno in my throat. Even Nonno's grappa doesn't go down as fiery. But then, I've never sculled the grappa.

Bahmir and Magda stand with their glasses, taking small cautious sips and shaking their heads at me.

'Hot! Fire water!' I utter through a fog of tears. 'That's what my nonno calls this stuff in Italian.'

Tracey looks at me like she doesn't get it, then laughs. 'Hot? Yeah, it is kind of hot, I guess.'

I grin. Stupid! The last of the great masters of the English language, that's me. Mum would love it. Paul Taranto, rich and superbly intelligent.

I wanted to hang around Tracey's place for a lot longer after I got used to taking short sharp sips of the whisky and after we'd had a few rounds of pool, but Tracey's parents arrived unexpectedly and she bundled Bahmir, Magda and me out the back door.

'My folks don't like strangers in the house when they're out,' Tracey says as I try for a kiss on her lips but plant one on her nose instead.

I'm a bit light-headed but manage to give Tracey a huge wave just before she slams the gate shut and I hear her running back towards the house.

'You want to come down to Rocco's?' asks Bahmir, his arms around Magda. 'Bet Dan'll still be there.'

I look around. It's not quite dark but it's getting close.

'Nah,' I say slowly. 'I'd better get back to my zia's place.' I have to get Nonno ready for when Mum comes by to pick us up. We're having pizza for dinner, after all. When I stop to think about it, pizza doesn't seem so appealing right now.

Bahmir gives me a high-five and he and Magda turn to go when I stop them.

'Hey, what do you reckon Tracey meant by her folks not wanting strangers around?' I ask suddenly. 'We're not strangers, are we?'

Bahmir shrugs. Magda pouts, then says, 'Tracey's old man is super sensitive. Tracey reckons he wants to meet all her friends before he lets her bring them home.'

'Oh,' I say and nod as Bahmir and Magda walk off in the opposite direction to me. I have a sudden thought and call out, 'Hey, Magda, have *you* met Tracey's folks?' But Magda doesn't answer.

On the walk back to Zia's I make a mental note to remind myself that Dan will just have to get used to the fact that a beautiful girl like Tracey can be mesmerised by someone like Paul Taranto. She did let me into her parents' house without their permission, didn't she? I also make a mental note to ask Tracey if she has any friends outside of school who might consider double-dating with us. I don't like my chances but, seeing as how Tracey is new to the neighbourhood and all.

It's well past dark by the time I round the corner into Zia Rita's street. The first of the street lights are on, and I know I'm in for a lecture when I get in. Still, it's worth a bit of an earbashing to have had so much time with Tracey. When the other guys find out I've spent almost an entire Saturday with her they'll be drooling with envy. Beautiful!

'Where have you *been*?'

I hear Mum's voice behind me, on the opposite footpath. Very odd.

'I asked you a question, Paul. Where have you been?'

I want to grin and say something really witty like, I've been to heaven with an angel, but it sounds pathetic even to me.

There's someone with Mum. It's Constable Movies. I recognise him straight away. He's not in his uniform, but he has got a large torch in one hand.

'Out looking for possums?' I say with a cheery smile, because I don't want a scene in front of the police, on-duty or off.

'Do you know what time it is?' asks Mum.

I look at my watch. I'm not wearing one. I show Mum my naked wrists.

Mum shakes her head. 'Well, at least we've found you,' she says firmly. 'That's something.'

'It's all right, Teresa. It'll be okay.' Constable Movies is looking up and down the street as though maybe there might be a traffic congestion he needs to clear.

'Mum?' I ask. 'Mum, what's going on?'

Mum comes and puts an arm around me and that's when I know for sure that something is wrong. It's not that Mum never puts her arms around me, it's the different ways she has of doing it that I'm up to speed on. And this is not one of those 'come here and give your poor mum a cuddle' types.

And this isn't quite the same as when she came in to tell me about Dad's accident either, but . . .

'Nonno's missing,' Mum says.

12

'Nonno can't be missing!' I snap. 'He's with Zia Rita. I left him there. On the couch.'

'What time was that, Paul?'

I look at Constable Movies.

'Paul? Do you know where Nonno might have gone?'

I look at Mum.

Just then Zia Rita comes running down the street from her driveway. She's in distress because I can see she hasn't bothered to apply the face trowel. Her eyes look all ghostly and her skin is pasty.

'Where have you *been*, Paul?' she asks.

'The track,' I answer. 'With Dan and Bahmir. Racing. I *told* you.' I look at Mum. 'I told you I had to race this afternoon.'

'Doesn't matter right now,' cuts in Constable Movies. 'If the old man didn't go with Paul, and he's not anywhere where you thought he might be, we have to figure out a more focused search pattern.'

Mum puts her hands on my shoulders and holds me out at arm's distance. 'There wasn't any more talk about homes and retirement villages was there, Paul? You and Zia didn't talk about any of that within his hearing just by chance, did you?'

'I've already told you we didn't!' snaps Zia Rita. 'Can't you trust me on that?'

'Like I trusted you to look after Dad for just a few hours?' Mum's voice is strained. I know she's scared.

'For mercy's sake, Teresa. There was no talk about homes or villages. But maybe if you hadn't been so stubborn in the past about not putting him into care, Dad *could* have been safe and sound somewhere. Cared for by professionals who are trained to cope with people like him . . .'

Zia Rita is huffing and shifting her weight from foot to foot.

'Paid professionals, Rita,' Mum says it so heatedly that her voice crackles. 'Not *family*, Rita. Not his own daughters!'

I try not to, but a long sigh hisses from my mouth. 'I should have been home with him,' I say, and mean it. 'He listens to me.'

Instead I was with Tracey Reynolds.

Formula 1 racing ace and English language guru, Paul 'The Don' Taranto, blamed for his Nonno's mysterious disappearance. The mega-star's girlfriend, Ms Tracey Reynolds, shattered by the news that now threatens to

98

destroy their blossoming relationship. Family goes into hiding.

I want to wind back the hours so that I get home before Nonno wakes up, so that I'm there for him. But I can't. Just like I couldn't when Dad died.

I know what's happened. Nonno has woken up, looked around, found himself in unfamiliar surroundings, forgotten he's at Zia Rita's, and bolted. Probably figured we'd done a swifty on him while he was asleep and dropped him off somewhere.

'He'll be panicked,' I say to no one in particular.

Mum has a pained look on her face. Her mouth is all tight and pale and thin.

'He'll be okay, Mum,' I try. 'He won't have gone too far.' But I don't know if even I believe that. Nonno is pretty resourceful when he wants to be. I mean, he did try to take a Porsche because he thought it was going to rain. The fact that it was just a model is sort of irrelevant in his mind, I reckon.

Mum suggests we contact the police again and Constable Movies gives her a blank stare.

'Of course,' Mum whispers. 'You've already told them.'

'I suggest some strong coffee,' Constable Movies announces officially and nods at Zia Rita. 'That okay by you?' he asks.

Zia Rita nods and the three of them turn towards her house.

'Aren't we going to keep looking?' I say more loudly than I intend. 'We can't just sit and have coffee and hope Nonno's going to come knocking on the door . . .'

'We've already looked in all the places we thought he might be,' Mum says. 'We even went back to our place, hoping maybe he'd found his way back there somehow.'

'So, we look again.' I know my voice is starting to rise but I can't help myself. I guess I'm angry with Mum and Zia, but I'm angrier with myself. Mum and Zia are always fighting about Nonno and what to do with him, but Nonno relies on me to keep him steady and level. It's my fault he woke up and decided whatever it was he decided. I bet he thought that I'd abandoned him.

I feel a thick lump in my throat.

Someone was supposed to have been with Dad when he had his accident. There was supposed to have been someone else there, near the crane, looking out for him. But there wasn't. And Dad got killed.

People should be there looking out for someone else when they're supposed to. That's the way it is.

Mum never said so, but Nonno's told me a hundred times that Dad should never have died. If there had been someone there for him like there was meant to be, chances are I'd still have my dad.

But I don't.

And now I don't have Nonno.

And a lot of that's my fault. I should have been back way earlier. Way, way earlier.

I don't wait to be told what to do. I'm running even before I've figured out where I'm running to. I round the corner with Mum's voice calling in my ears for me to stop, but I don't. I bolt straight for the railway cutting, down one of the stormwater pipes that passes under a footbridge and leads back towards our place. Then I hot-foot it across the Safeway carpark and down a lane that forks out in two different directions at the end, one of which runs into our street.

I guess I didn't really expect to find Nonno at home, and I don't find him there. It was just a faint hope that Nonno might have somehow made his way back after Mum had been to check. Why didn't one of them stay here in case he did return? But I suppose that's what happens when people panic.

'Where would an old man hide?' I don't answer myself because I don't know. And even if I did I wouldn't answer out loud. People get put away for having conversations with themselves. Nonno tells me that every time I catch him talking to himself and ask him what he's doing.

Nothing, he'll say.

Crap. You're talking to yourself, I'll tell him.

Rubbish. People wot talk to himself get himself locked up.

Nonno always laughs at that. I can't ever quite figure out if he's laughing at himself or at me.

If he was here now though I'd let him talk to himself all he wanted. I'd even let him forget my name like he does sometimes and not pick him up on it.

It's dark outside and the moon is dull, but luckily it's a balmy sort of night so at least Nonno won't be huddled somewhere shivering with cold.

I tell myself that as I walk back to the bedroom I share with him.

Things could be worse.

Nonno could be . . .

Don't be stupid, Don Paul Taranto. If you don't get a grip you'll come up with all sorts of crazy ideas about what might be happening to Nonno.

And I figure if Mum and Zia have already checked out all the places we might usually find Nonno hiding, there's really only one place for me to be. That's right here in my . . . *our* bedroom. I have to be here. When Nonno comes back someone has to be here to make sure he *stays* here.

I feel embarrassed sitting in the dark on my bed. Embarrassed for running off from Mum the way I did. I should give her a ring at Zia's and tell her I'm here and that I'm staying for when Nonno turns up. It was a pretty stupid thing running off like I did. I mean, where was I going anyway but back here? I could have got Mum to drive me back.

'Why'd you go and leave for?' I ask the crate marked *Mildura Oranges – Fresh and Delicious. R.*

Trotter & Sons. Nonno's crate. The one he tells me he brought out from Italy with him. The one packed with all his personal stuff.

I've never taken much notice of just how battered the old crate is. Battered but solid, like it was built to house important stuff. I guess if you're an orange grower then oranges are pretty important stuff. It has a lid fixed to it with rusty hinges. A wooden lid Nonno puts his false teeth on when he sleeps. It's where Nonno keeps his precious aftershave bottles, rows of them, all shapes and sizes and colours. He has a thing about aftershave. Nonno has to have aftershave at hand all the time. He can't bear to find that he's run out. I know, because as a joke I once substituted water for his current favourite and he went ballistic. Nonno carried on as though I'd bashed him or something. He started yelling and crying, and it took Mum ages to settle him down.

I was scared shitless. It was the only time I've ever been scared of Nonno. His face was all contorted, and he was trembling all over.

I've never touched his bottles again. Not even as a joke. I even put up with him waking up in the middle of the night sometimes and cleaning them with his hanky. Another quirk in Nonno's nature, I guess. Something else I'll continue to overlook if he'd *just come back*.

Nonno's never said so, but I reckon he put the lid on that crate himself, and the brass lock.

I fiddle with the lock the way I have done a million times before. The aftershave bottles shake and clink together, so I stop and plonk myself down in front of the crate and screw up my nose.

Please come home, Nonno. *Please*.

13

Dan might be a bit thick sometimes, but he's a real mate. He's going to scout the neighbourhood again looking for Nonno, soon as he can get away from the house.

I've tried Tracey Reynolds's place too, but the girl who answered the phone came back on the line and told me Tracey had a headache and wasn't taking any calls for the rest of the weekend. Tracey must have the most savage headache of all time. I've left a message for her to call me when she feels up to it.

It's been almost two hours since I was told about Nonno, and still no news. Constable Movies is out in the kitchen with Mum who packed it when I took off like I did from outside Zia Rita's. Apparently Constable Movies got it in one where I'd run off to. Must be a cop 'sixth sense' or something. I'm still not too keen on him hanging around, but I have to give him credit for the way he handled Mum when she burst in and found me sitting in the dark by Nonno's crate. She was right out of her tree. Said that she had enough to worry about with Nonno missing and she didn't need me running off like a lunatic. Constable Movies calmed her down: reminded her that I was just trying to help. That I was probably feeling bad about the whole thing and wouldn't it be better if she just waited for news from the police and others who were out looking for Nonno.

When I suggested I should be out there searching too, now that there was someone home to wait for Nonno, Mum gave me her 'don't you dare even *think* about leaving this house' look.

That's why I phoned Dan. I need to feel like I'm doing something.

I sit by the bedroom window and stare out at the night. Saturday night. I think of Nonno and where he might be. He could be anywhere. Mum even thought Nonno might have made his way to the Italian Club. But he wasn't at the Club, and no one there had seen him. Not since Wednesday when he came home with the Porsche.

Jeez, Nonno is an odd bloke. Like, sometimes at night when I think we're both asleep, I'll suddenly hear the window open and I'll catch Nonno having a drag of a cigarette, blowing smoke into the night air. Mum doesn't want him to smoke, especially because he has a weak heart and his lungs aren't what they use to be. I should stop him. I know I should. But I don't. Nonno's an old man. Mum keeps reminding me that he's been through heaps, even a world war when he was just a kid. So I can't see the point of denying him a cigarette now.

It would be strange to come to bed at night and not have to listen to Nonno mumble under his breath in his sleep. But at least I'd have the entire room to myself. That'd be cool. I could chuck my stuff around like Dan does in his room. I could have the entire desk to myself even. Without Nonno's bed crowding the space I could probably get myself one of those new DVD players, a bean bag, maybe even a set of wild speakers!

It would be so cool. My own room. All mine.

But not like this.

Nonno always says that one day soon he'll be gone and then . . .

I have a sudden thought. I have a few of those. Out of the blue thoughts.

Today is Saturday. That means tomorrow is Sunday.

'Where's my diary?' I'm talking to myself but that's okay. This is an emergency.

My school diary should be in my school bag. That's logical. It's not there, though. My school diary is still at school, in my desk. I think.

'Calendar. I need a calendar.'

I go to the desk Nonno and I share. My side is stacked with books, note paper, comics, trading cards, CDs, bits and pieces of model aircraft I've never got round to finishing, and probably a few old sandwiches I never quite got through. Nonno's side has a vase with a plastic rose in it, an old cigar box with his loose change in it, and one solitary CD of opera arias he insisted on buying about three years ago. He loves that CD. Plays it on my portable whenever I'm around to load it for him. And he's got a pocket calendar . . .

I fumble the pages but finally find what I'm searching for. Nonno has marked the first Sunday of each month with a red pencil.

'Tomorrow is the first Sunday of the month,' I hear myself say.

'Mum!' I yell. 'Mum! I think I know where Nonno is.'

I run from our bedroom into the kitchen, expecting to see Mum there. She's not. Constable Movies isn't, either.

The back door is open and I spot Mum in the garden. She's alone, her arms folded across her chest.

Something tells me she wants to be on her own right now.

She's been through a lot too, my mum. And I don't just mean today. I mean with Dad dying suddenly. Nonno's health. Fights with Zia Rita about Nonno and what to do with him if he gets any worse. And I guess I haven't exactly been easy to live with.

So I don't disturb Mum. Nonno is my responsibility. I was the one who abandoned him. I should have stayed with him at Zia Rita's. At least until I was sure he was okay there.

I go back to my room, grab what I think I'll need and scribble a note to Mum which I leave on the kitchen table. Then I'm out the front door. I turn left and sprint up the street on the opposite side, just in case Constable Movies is out and about.

Tracey Reynolds pops into my head. Probably because I'm running flat out and she is such an athlete.

I wish she had managed to get over her headache enough to give me a call. Must be a *really* bad headache to keep her in bed on a Saturday night.

I tell myself to remember to get her a card, something funny, maybe even a little rude, to cheer her up. I could take it in to her tomorrow. Drop by her place once everything with Nonno settles. Girls like the personal touch. Dan told me his eldest sister Ruth was bowled over when her boyfriend appeared one day at their front door with a dozen red roses – and it wasn't even Ruth's birthday or anything.

You're different, Paul Taranto, that's what Tracey said. I'm different. Jeez, like Nonno really. He's sort of different. The Don. That's who he is. Don Nonno.

Like, I don't know anyone else who has a Nonno who has already bought his own burial plot and tends it like a garden.

Nonno has bought himself a huge plot at the city cemetery. A double plot. He told Mum that he wants the space. He doesn't want to feel cramped in. Mum was shocked. I laughed. Sure it sounded weird, but it made sense to Nonno. And Nonno's plot isn't far from Dad.

Nonno and I tend the plots together the first Sunday of every month. Just me and him. We weed and clean Dad's grave first, and place fresh flowers in all the concrete vases, then we potter around Nonno's plot.

It's high on a slope, Nonno's plot, surrounded on three sides by huge cypress trees and on the other there is a small open courtyard with a fountain that runs water all day and all night.

Nonno made me laugh when he told me he hoped the constant sound of running water wouldn't keep him awake.

I don't tell Mum Nonno's jokes because she'd get all upset. I get upset too, sometimes. Nonno's like that. He can get me upset by doing or saying the most stupid things. And he can be a real nuisance. But still I don't want Nonno to die for a long time yet.

I wonder if Tracey Reynolds's family have their own plots. They're probably rich enough to have a whole crypt to themselves. Probably rich enough to have themselves frozen and stored until someone can figure out a way to bring them back to life.

I know Dad's never coming back. Mum reckons

Dad hasn't really gone completely. As long as I keep thinking about him, Dad will always be there. But thoughts can hurt too. I'm thinking so much I don't realise where I am until I get to the gates of the cemetery. It's an old place, so the gates don't lock properly and it gives without much effort.

And that's when I stop and think about where I am.

The light from the torch I've grabbed from under my bed is not as strong as I'd like. In a cemetery I'd want to have total flood lighting, like they do at the Melbourne Cricket Ground and other big sports stadiums. Enough light so that you can fool yourself that it's actually the middle of the day and there aren't any ghosts and ghouls and walking dead lurking in the shadows.

I wonder whether Dad would recognise me. I mean, do you lose your memory and stuff once you're dead? I don't know. I hope not.

I've been coming here so often that I even know the shortcuts to Nonno's plot. Even in the dark I know where the fountain is . . .

'Nonno?'

It has to be him, huddled on the rim of the fountain. I shine the light from the torch in his face. Nonno blinks and lifts a hand to shield his eyes. He's eating, his mouth stuffed.

'I knew you'd be here,' I say, relieved. There's a lump in my throat. I didn't want to admit it, but I didn't know what I was going to do if Nonno hadn't been here.

'We've been worried sick about you!' I add a little angrily and plonk myself down next to him, giving Nonno the once-over. He looks okay. He's brought the bag of pistachio nuts with him he took to Zia Rita's house. 'What're you doing here? Why'd you run off from Zia's for?'

'Sheeps,' Nonno whispers and grins at me. I see bits of pistachio nuts dribble out of his mouth.

'What?'

'Sheeps,' Nonno repeats and touches the side of his nose with a finger.

I shake my head. Nonno can be so frustrating. But I'm happy enough to have found him not to bother too much trying to make sense of what he's saying.

'You want to go home?' I ask and sweep the light from the torch in a wide arc around our feet. 'It's too quiet here.'

'I not find enni sheeps,' Nonno starts sadly. 'I look evriwhere but I not find even one sheeps. I veri sorry, Paul. I try but . . .' Nonno shrugs and holds out a handful of pistachio nuts to me.

He's a great bloke really, my nonno. But now, listening to him tell me how he went looking for sheep in the heart of a city like Melbourne, I'm scared suddenly. Scared that maybe Zia Rita is right. Maybe Nonno does need special care now. Maybe Nonno *is* becoming a danger to himself. I mean, he did just wander off. Mum lets him go to the Italian Club and stuff, and even last year he came with me to the footy now and then, but . . .

'Sorry I wasn't there when you woke up,' I say. I try to repeat myself in Nonno's Italian dialect but three words in and I'm lost. 'I thought Zia Rita and you could talk maybe . . .' My turn to shrug.

Cemeteries are so quiet. You'd have to be a real moron to think that they're jumping with music and stuff. It's just that right now, right at this moment as I sit next to my nonno and I listen to the soft sound of the nuts grinding under his false teeth, there doesn't seem to be any other sound in the entire world. Just the crrk . . . crrk . . . crrk of the nuts being ground.

'You ghelfriend,' Nonno says suddenly. 'I wos try get the sheeps for you to give to hims father. Like I done it hwuen I wos chase after you nonna in Italy.' Nonno snorts and spits. 'I give to you nonna father three sheeps.' Nonno holds up four fingers, then slowly bends one down to show three. 'I walk here, there, round and up, and after while I not can find which way is for go back Rita house. Dat why I come here. Here I unnerstand how to come. After me too tired for walk back our house straight way so I wait for morning come.' Nonno grins at me. 'Den you come take me home!'

'You went looking for sheep for Tracey's dad?'

Nonno nods. 'Dat him name? Tratcy. Nice name. I like it.'

I stare hard at Don Nonno. He left Zia Rita's and went out alone looking for sheep. I feel the tears in my eyes and clear my throat.

The anger of a few minutes before disappears.

'*Her* name, Nonno. Tracey is a girl. Girls are "her", boys are "him". Capisci?' I whisper.

Nonno cuts the air with both hands and pulls his mouth into a thin line. 'I too old for learn nuther linguich!' he snaps. 'I look for him sheeps but I not can find one! Sorry. Maibe you give to Tratcy father someting wot is good liek sheeps.'

'How about a model Porsche?' I say gently.

Nonno didn't run away at all. He went out looking for sheep. Sheep for me to give to Tracey's old man as a kind of . . . I don't know . . . a dowry, I guess. Like people used to do in Nonno's Monte Sereno back in Italy.

I'm relieved and scared at the same time. Relieved because Nonno hadn't been trying to run away. Scared because he really seems to believe I need sheep.

'Romina's not here!' Nonno says suddenly in Italian. 'My beautiful Romina isn't here!'

I lean forward and touch Nonno lightly on the arm. The way I do when he wakes at night and starts talking to my dead nonna, and I have to get him settled again.

'Nonna Romina's in Italy,' I say. 'You remember? She wanted to be sent back to your village when she . . .' I don't say the word.

'I can't bring it to her the flowers,' Nonno tells me, in English now, his voice quivering. 'I can't come say, "I love you like hwuen we wos first marry." I have to send back to Italy my beautiful Romina.'

Nonno draws a shallow breath and looks around. Then he looks back at me. 'I do what she asked me to do, Paolo,' Nonno says in Italian. 'When Romina died I sent her back to her family. But I did it with a broken heart because I am her family, too. Me, and you, and your mother. And Rita. But Romina was never really happy here. She came to Australia for *me*. To be with *me*. When she died I sent her back. It was the least I could do after all she did for me.' Nonno lowers his voice. 'You understand, Paolo?'

I reach across and hug Nonno. I feel him heave slightly under my arm.

'I can't bring her flowers.' Nonno pauses. Then he continues slowly, still in Italian. 'There was a flower, a rose, on Romina's wedding ring. A little rose. On the inside of the band. I haven't seen it for so long. I let her take it with her. So maybe, maybe my Romina always has flowers, eh?'

Nonno swallows slowly. 'One little flower, Paolo. I can't bring her any more flowers. But . . .' Nonno goes on. 'But I can smell nice for her!' Nonno looks at me. 'I smell nice, Paul?' he asks me in English. 'I not smell like a goat no more, eh?'

I nod. 'You don't smell like a goat. Or a sheep even.

You always smell nice.' I get to my feet. I help Nonno to his feet. 'Let's go home, Nonno.'

Nonno shuffles. 'No need come back tomorrow,' he tells me. 'While I wos wait for you to come I clean you papa grave already, and mine too!'

I nod. I grin. Sometimes Nonno doesn't remember my name. Sometimes he doesn't even remember that he has any children of his own. And then sometimes he remembers every tiny detail about Nonna Romina and his life with her, and how he sent her body back to Italy for burial in Monte Sereno, and how much it hurt him to do that. How much it still hurts him.

Nonno surprises me . . . again and again.

14

By the time Nonno and I got back home it was almost dawn. Mum was rapt to see us walk in the door. She grabbed and hugged us both as though we'd just got off a plane at Tulla airport after being away for a year. Constable Movies told me he had to physically stop Mum from chasing after me when she found my scribbled note I'd left on the kitchen table.

I guess I should be thankful for that much.

Constable Movies told me he thought a boy my age should be given a chance to prove himself. So that's why he let me go. Fact is, Mum didn't come running to the cemetery, and Nonno and me did get back home okay. Tired, but okay.

It's almost midday before I get out of bed. I look over and am glad to see Nonno is still asleep. I roll out of bed quietly. I don't want to disturb him.

In the kitchen Mum plants a kiss on my forehead and nods for me to sit.

'I don't understand,' she says, putting a late breakfast before me. 'I don't understand why your nonno says he was out looking for sheep yesterday.'

I take a long gulp of the beaten egg Mum has blended with a dash of marsala in a cup. 'He told you about the sheep?' I ask, but I don't look at Mum. Good one, Nonno.

'Your nonno said something about needing to find sheep. For you.' I see Mum's shadow on the table. 'What's this all about, Paul?'

I sip some more egg. I scratch a sudden itch.

'I must have told Nonno that I need to get a sheep's heart for a biology prac at school,' I say finally. 'I guess he thought I wanted him to get the whole sheep for me. Sorry.'

I don't want to have to look at Mum's eyes. I hate it when she seems to see right through me. I'm doing my best to bore a hole in the plate instead.

'I don't know what gets into you sometimes, Paul,' Mum sighs.

I shrug. I really don't want to get into all the detail about Tracey and how Nonno reckons I need to give her dad sheep.

Mum goes to the sink.

'Oh, by the way, Dan Declan came by while you were still asleep,' she says.

Dan! I had meant to call him first thing! I wanted to thank him for going out to look for Nonno.

Mum taps the sink gently with the tips of her fingers.

'He asked me to give you this.' Mum reaches into her pocket and pulls out a folded note. She holds it out to me. 'Don't worry, I haven't read it.'

I take the note and find that it's been sticky taped shut.

'Must be some super-extra-secret message for Dan to have sticky taped it closed like that,' Mum says and raises her eyebrows.

I stare at the folded sheet of paper.

Mum stands and watches me watch the folded sheet of paper.

'Aren't you going to read it?' she asks.

I shrug. Why would Dan bring me a folded note?

'Sheep's hearts . . . secret notes. You boys are a real worry sometimes, Paul,' Mum calls over her shoulder as she turns to grab a jar of tomato paste from the fridge.

Nonno shuffles in just then. He's holding an empty aftershave bottle in each hand and trying to hold onto his walking-stick as well.

'You and Nonno both,' Mum adds and walks out.

'Hwuen I wos young man I not hiave enough money for buy aftershave,' Nonno says without hesitation to no one in particular. 'I hiave to go visit my Romina smelling like one goat.' Nonno sighs and looks at me. 'I make to myself promise dat when I got money I always smell nice. Always. Even when me old and stupid in the head.'

'You're not stupid in the head,' I say, hoping Nonno will wander off into the backyard.

'But I old,' he grins. 'Old, but I smell good! True or not?'

I nod. That's one thing about Nonno. No matter what time of day he always smells fresh. Always has as far as I can remember.

'What're you doing with those bottles?' I ask, hoping that maybe he's finally clearing up the top of his crate.

Nonno stares at both bottles a moment, then holds one out to me. 'I wos remember when you nonna Romina she tell me how she like dis aftershave.' He grins, holds out the other bottle, steadying himself on his walking-stick. 'I wos think when you give to me dis aftershave. You wos so little I wos hold you on my lap and let you play my piano accordion.'

I blink at Nonno. He blinks back at me. I don't remember giving him that bottle of aftershave. I probably did, except that sometimes he invents the past.

Mum says sometimes he's filling in the gaps, but Nonno seems to remember heaps about long ago pretty well. It's more recent stuff he forgets so easily. That and my name, and who Mum is, and . . .

Guess I do that too, sometimes. Fill in the gaps. Like when I think of Dad and imagine that me and him have been out playing kick-to-kick, or he's watched me go-carting. Or I've asked him what he thinks about girls, because everyone who knew him reckons Dad was a real lady-killer.

I shake my head.

Some things are too hard, even to imagine.

I get up and walk out into the backyard, plonk down against the fence between our place and the apartment block next door, and prise open Dan's message.

I read: *I'm glad you found The Don.*

And that's it.

I turn the paper over but there's nothing on the other side.

Strange, but then Dan can be strange when he wants to be.

'Paul!'

'Outside!'

Mum comes to the back door. She isn't alone. Constable Movies is with her. He's not in uniform. He looks even younger than when he was standing beside the grumpy older cop the day Nonno got busted over the Porsche. Not a good sign.

'Wayne just dropped by on his way to work to see how you and Nonno are,' Mum says by way of explanation.

Wayne.

Now it's *Wayne*, is it?

I guess I shouldn't be surprised. Even Dan reckons my mum is attractive for a mum. And Mum and Constable Movies did go to the movies together the other night. What did I expect Mum to call him, Constable Movies?

'Nonno and me are great,' I say shortly and get to my feet.

'Glad to hear that, Paul,' Constable Wayne . . . No, don't like the ring of that. Constable Movies sounds way better.

Constable Movies runs a hand over his spiky head and grins in my direction.

'That was pretty smart of you to figure out where your grandfather was,' he smiles and looks sideways at Mum. Mum grins at her feet like some of the girls at school do. 'You might consider becoming a police officer when you finish school. The force can always use bright people like you.'

Sounds like a scene from *Star Wars*. The Force be with you, and you.

I don't say anything. What can I say? Hey, thanks for the vocational counselling? You've really helped me sort out my ambitions?

One of those awkward silences falls over us.

Nonno, who is just behind Mum, smiles at me and pulls a face. I grin and look at my hands. When I look up again Nonno is barring his teeth the way I've seen baboons do on those TV docos about African wildlife they show at school as part of Sexuality Week. Only Nonno isn't screeching or scratching at himself.

'I'd better get going, Teresa,' Constable Movies

says and waves at me. I nod my head in reply. When Constable Movies turns round he jumps a little to find Nonno standing there.

'I not take Porsche,' Nonno says deadpan and shows his bottles as proof.

Mum mumbles something and pushes Constable Movies back indoors. Nonno nods and smiles and holds his empty aftershave bottles close to his chest. Nonno steps out carefully into the backyard.

'You papa would be happy see Teresa smiling again,' he says.

'Yeah, right,' I manage. Seeing Mum even remotely interested in a man other than Dad makes my stomach twist.

'You father wos love you mama, Paul,' Nonno goes on. 'Him wos say all time he wos lucky man hiave you mama.'

'But he's gone now,' I say.

Nonno shrugs. 'Lot people gone. You papa. My Romina. One day, me too. Is Life.'

'You sure you don't want to go clean up the plot today?' I ask. 'I left the afternoon open on purpose like always. First Sunday of the month, remember?'

'I clean him yesterday night,' Nonno replies. With some effort Nonno balances the bottles in one arm and reaches into the pocket of his waistcoat with his free hand, his walking-stick on the crook of his arm.

He holds a closed fist out in my direction, turns his

hand over and over, keeping his fist tightly clenched.

'What're you doing?'

Nonno narrows his eyes. 'Magic!' he grins.

I groan. Nonno's magic consists of taking a coin and making it 'appear' behind one of my ears. Unconsciously I rub a spot behind my right ear.

'I had to let go Romina when she died,' Nonno goes on. 'And hwuen she want be buried back in Italy I hiave to agree. Not because I not want my wife be bury here, but because me love my wife and even when she dead I want make sure she be happy.'

I've heard it before. When Nonna Romina died suddenly about twelve years ago she left strict instructions that she wanted her body returned to Monte Sereno in Italy for burial. Much to all his friends' amazement, Nonno did as Nonna Romina wished. But to everyone's astonishment, so Mum told me after Dad died, Nonno said that when he dies he wants to be buried in Australia. That's why he's bought a plot already, because he wants to be sure.

Nonno opens his hand and winks at me. There's a small brass key lying in the palm of his hand. It looks like a letterbox key, or a locker key.

'This is a magic key,' Nonno beams in Italian and pinches the key between two fingers. 'This key is *very* special.'

'Looks a bit small to be the key to a Ferrari,' I say half jokingly.

'Bah, Ferrari!' Nonno snaps, and for the first time in a while he looks angry. His fist slaps shut and he pockets the key again. 'I wos tink you ready, but you not,' he says with a shake of his head.

'Ready for what?' I ask and have to follow Nonno who has turned and is walking back into the house. 'For crying out loud, Nonno, what are you going on about now?'

Nonno pauses and stomps the butt of his walking-stick down. He looks at me over his shoulder.

'Ready for anyting, good and bad. No more talk, now. *Basta!*' Nonno says and arches his eyebrows and flares his nostrils so that I'm not sure if he's mad . . . or just, mad!

Then he's gone.

I sort of want to chase him and get him to talk sense but then I think what's the point. Nonno is stubborn enough not to utter another word for the entire day if that's what he's decided to do.

Sometimes Nonno gets me so angry I want to side with Zia Rita about taking him to a home.

15

Nonno can't be left alone in the bath. The last time Mum and me did leave him alone he tried to shave his private parts. We had to get the local doctor to come over and patch him up. It was heaps embarrassing, but more than that, it was frightening. I won't ever forget the sight of Nonno lying there in the bath, the water turning a pale pink with his blood and him looking up at me as though nothing unusual had happened. *Wot problem you got?* he'd said to me casually.

His comment almost made me laugh. Almost. My nonno is a proud man.

So I'm sitting beside the bath in front of the plastic curtain that's around it, sitting on a stool Nonno made when he could still hold an adze and a hammer.

'You almost done in there?' I ask, getting bored. I yawn loudly. It's Sunday night. I'm still tired from last night and besides, Sunday night is card night. Me and

Nonno, one on one. He loves it, even when he forgets to play a hand.

Nonno is whistling. I know the tune. It's very old, like eighty years or something. I recognise it because Nonno whistles it every time he has a bath. He reckons he can remember his mother humming the song to him when he was a little boy back in Monte Sereno, back before the war and the bombs and the destruction he tells us about sometimes.

'You wos drink yesterday, yes,' Nonno says suddenly. I stiffen.

'I know because my nose like the dog nose wot can sniff the dead people which is in the rumble of the buildings,' Nonno adds.

I'm stunned. Not even Mum picked up on the whisky that must have been on my breath the night before. Or if she did she hasn't mentioned it. Yet.

'You're dreaming,' I go, and watch his faint silhouette shift on the curtain.

'No, me no dream,' Nonno peeks out from behind the curtain and grins. 'See, look. Me awake.'

'Yeah, yeah, whatever.'

'I remember hwuen I wos boy . . .' Here we go again. I roll my eyes. '. . . I take it my father's vino wot him make and me and my friends we drink till we cannot stand,' Nonno goes on. 'We drink and laugh and more we drink more we laugh until we fall on ground and go sleep. I not know how long we sleeps but must be too long because it wos my father wot finds us and him not hiappi at all wot him find.' Nonno laughs and splashes water. 'I wos much curiosity for drink the vino like a man, but I not man enough yet at dat time and so I wos be sick for two or three days.'

'We don't make wine any more, remember?' I try. 'Not since Dad died.'

There is more water splashing. Nonno loves the sound of water splashing. He says it's a beautiful sound because when he was a boy he had to walk for miles to get water from a well.

'I not say you be drink you *papa's* vino,' Nonno says through the plip plop of his farting in the water. 'I wos say you wos drink yesterday. I not stupido of this things.'

I shrug. 'So what. It was just to try the stuff . . .'

'I not say you wrong,' Nonno continues. 'I not say you right. I joust say I can smell it the drink on you mouth. Dat all wot I say.'

'So why make a big deal about it, then?' I can feel myself getting annoyed with Nonno and try to end the conversation. It's like he knows stuff about me and what I do, and what I think sometimes, too.

Nonno pulls the curtain back again and squints out at me. His face is red and blotchy, his eyes yellowed, and his few strands of hair are limp across his scalp. He is holding the blue sponge I gave him last Fathers' Day, along with a bottle of aftershave and bath salts.

'Because I love you very much, Paul,' he says seriously. 'I wos know you find me yesterday because me and you we same in so much ways. Not joust for try the drink, no. Much more stronger than dis.' Nonno reaches out and drips water all over Mum's clean floor. He touches me gently on the chest, his fingertips leaving tiny damp patches on my shirt.

'I wos scare when I wos sit there all alone in the cemetery,' Nonno says, still holding my gaze. 'I wos walk evriwhere look for the sheeps for you ghelfriend Tratcy, and I got lost.' He sniffs loudly, then adds in Italian, 'It's funny. I couldn't find my way back here, to my home, but found my way to the cemetery. Don't you think this is funny, Paolo?'

I clear my throat. I hate it when Nonno gets all emotional like this. I get all knotted up inside. *Paul Taranto, whisky drinker, Formula 1 racing ace and English language guru, taken to hospital with insides wrapped round kitchen fork. Young star's nonno explains how it's done.*

'Come on,' I say before I really choke, 'here's your towel.' I stand and open the towel out at full stretch so that Nonno can step into it. Only he doesn't. Nonno pulls the plug from the bath instead and sits watching the water swirl down the plughole.

'You're going to get sucked down into the drains,' I warn. 'Then Mum is really going to kick my arse.'

Nonno laughs. 'I like hiave bath my own home,' he says softly, without looking at me.

'Course you do. Where else do you expect to take a bath? With Susan next door? I'm sure she'd love that, eh.' I step forward and rub the towel over Nonno's head. He lets me pat his shoulders and neck dry.

'She veri sexy!' Nonno says cheerily.

'Who?'

'The young ghel next door. The one wot you say I can go hiave the bath with.'

I laugh and towel dry Nonno's back. 'Dream on,' I tell him. The image of my nonno in the bath with the young woman next door flashes before my eyes. I cringe.

'I tink it be very cold when I die,' Nonno announces suddenly. 'I tink I want wear heavy suit. My dark blue one maibe. With my red tie and my waistcoat.'

I don't say anything. I don't like it when Nonno talks about his death.

'I tink best I wear it my blue suit when I die. Blue suit him keeps me warm. I not want be cold when I dead.' Nonno pauses and taps the side of his nose. 'You make sure they put to me the blue suit, Paul. I want look good for my Romina. She wait for me.' He stops, then adds, 'Make sure I smell nice, too. Must smell nice. Not like goats. Not like goats.'

'Shut up about dying. I reckon you'll outlive me and Mum and probably a heap of other people as well.' I say this but I know I don't believe it. I know Nonno knows I don't believe it.

I help Nonno to his feet, make sure he has the towel around him and step aside. Slowly Nonno steps out of the bath. With the towel draped around him he reminds me of the Roman emperors I've seen in movies about gladiators and the Easter Passion and all that stuff.

'I sorry I wos not find the sheeps for you,' Nonno whispers. 'I sorry I make you scare yesterday because you wos tink I wos lost.' Nonno's eyes are clouded. He has cataracts.

I swallow. 'Hey, no drama. Aussie girls prefer sheepdogs anyway.'

Nonno frowns. 'Sheepsdogs? Dis bloody strange country still.'

An hour later, after I've helped Nonno dress, and as he shuffles the deck of cards for our regular game of Scopa, Nonno turns to Mum and asks her to fetch his pipe from the stable where he thinks he's left it after milking the goats.

Mum looks at me and I can see she's upset. No matter how often Nonno falls back into the past as though it's the present, Mum just can't seem to get used to it.

'Romina,' Nonno says again, 'get me my pipe!'

I look at Mum. I keep looking at her to try and remind her that, like always, Nonno's hiccup with time and place will be over pretty soon. She's just got to hang in there. Trouble is, Nonno is doing this more and more lately, thinking Mum is Nonna Romina and I'm, well, sometimes I'm Nonno's best mate Giacomo. Other times I'm one of a hundred other people from Nonno's childhood.

'You stopped smoking ages ago, remember?' I say to Nonno because of Mum not knowing about Nonno sneaking a smoke out of our bedroom window every now and then.

Nonno sits back in his chair and stares at the cards in his hands. He nods. He narrows his eyes and taps the cards gently on the table. His eyes flicker for a second.

'I could have been a great singer,' he says quietly in his native Italian dialect, the way he always does when he's thinking about the long-ago past that is so clear in his mind. So much clearer than a lot of the present. 'I could have had a fabulous career. My voice. They said it was the voice of an angel itself. But the devil stole it all from me . . . The devil came and stole it all from me.'

When the phone rings in the hall I'm glad of the distraction. I don't bother to ask Nonno what he's going on about this time and I leave the kitchen table pretty fast.

'Hello?'

It's Tracey. She's feeling heaps better, although she did have to miss a training session this morning. She and Bahmir and Magda are going to catch a movie and want to know if I'll go, too.

I'm not allowed out on Sunday nights. Mum doesn't think I should be anywhere but at home getting ready for school the next day. And besides, Sunday night is card night with Nonno.

That's what I should tell Tracey.

'My nonno's pretty sick at the moment,' I say instead and feel bad about using my nonno as an excuse like that. But I do it anyway. 'Mum and me might have to take him to the doctor and stuff... Sorry... maybe another...'

'I'd really like to see you again, Don Paul,' Tracey whispers down the line.

I'd really like to see you too, I think. I'm trying really hard to remember if I actually did kiss Tracey the day before or whether I dreamt it. I'm not sure. Must be the whisky I sculled.

'I'm going to feel so lonely in that dark, dark cinema all by myself,' Tracey purrs. 'All alone while Magda has Bahmir to cuddle up to during all the scary bits and...'

'I'll be there in spirit,' I blurt out like some truly exceptional Neanderthal.

'What?'

'I wish I could sprint there.' I gag on the words. 'Right now. Sooner even, but...'

Nonno is beside me. I cover the mouthpiece. 'I'll be there in a sec,' I tell him.

'Is ghel, yes?' Nonno grins. 'Tell to him dat I wos try hard find the sheeps.' Nonno reaches out and before I can stop him he takes the phone and holds it to his ear and mouth.

'Allo, Tratcy. I look for the sheeps for you,' he says. 'Me is Paul nonno. You like Paul, yes?'

I grab at the phone, struggle with Nonno for a few moments before he steps back and blinks into my face.

'Can't you just mind your own business for a change!' I snap. 'Not everything has to involve *you*, okay?'

'Who was that?' Tracey asks as I hold the phone to my ear again and shoo Nonno away with my free hand. He stands there by the telephone, still blinking at me.

'Paul? Paul, you there?' asks Tracey down the line.

'Yeah . . .' I turn my back on Nonno. It's easier to ignore him that way.

'Who was that?' Tracey asks again.

'No one,' I lie. I feel fingertips prod my back but I refuse to look around.

Paul Taranto, major loser. Signed, Tracey Reynolds.

'Well, I'd be rapt if you could come meet us.' Tracey's voice is like cool vanilla icecream. I splutter and have to cough a few times to clear my throat.

I'd *kill* to go meet Tracey and catch a movie. And if the world was a fair place that's exactly what I'd be doing. But I can't go. I might be able to sneak out our bedroom window after pretending to get homework done, but I know that at some stage Nonno will come in.

Sometimes I really, really wish me and Nonno didn't have to share a bedroom.

'Sorry, Tracey, no can do,' I say slowly. This is not good. Not good at all. 'Hey, why don't we pick another night?'

Tracey doesn't commit to another night. She has training and stuff. And I don't really listen anyway, after she tells me she'll have to get back to me on it.

I slam down the phone before I can stop myself. Nonno's come back into the hall. 'Can't you just mind your own business sometimes?' I turn on him as I brush past.

'Who was that?' Mum asks as I return to the kitchen.

'Didn't *he* tell you?' I point at Nonno who's followed me.

Mum looks at Nonno. He shuffles over to the table and sits down, gathers up the cards and holds them palm down. He's ready to play another hand. I stare at him. I shake my head. He probably doesn't even remember what just happened. I feel a tinge of regret, but not enough to stop me telling him I've just remembered I've got homework to do and could he and Mum please not disturb me if they don't mind.

'Paul?'

I don't need to look at Mum to know she's staring at me with one of those 'you want to explain yourself' looks.

'What?' I say. I don't look at Nonno.

'What's the matter with you, Paul?' Mum asks.

What's the matter with me? I just passed on a chance to go to the movies with maybe the hottest girl in my year, that's what's the matter with me. I have to share a bedroom with an old man who can't remember what he had for dinner tonight but *can* bore you *senseless* with the names of every friend he ever had back during World War II, that's what's the matter with me. My mum is going out with the cop who came to arrest my nonno for borrowing a toy Porsche, that's what's the matter with me.

'Nothing's the matter with me,' I say as calmly as I can.

'You can't just walk out on your nonno like this, Paul,' Mum whispers, coming to stand in front of me. 'He's expecting you to play Scopa with him. One game of Scopa with your nonno, Paul. Surely you can spare ten minutes from your homework for that. You and Nonno play cards every Sunday night.'

I shrug. 'Well, maybe I don't want to play Scopa tonight, okay? Maybe we play cards too often.'

Mum touches me lightly on the chin. Her hand is soft. 'What's going on here, Paul?' she asks. 'Yesterday you were supposed to be taking care of Nonno and you took off to God knows where. Now you get some . . . some phone call, and you come in here all in a huff and announce you don't want to be disturbed because you suddenly have homework to do. What *is* it with you at the moment?'

'Zia Rita was supposed to be taking care of Nonno last night,' I say. 'But I guess we're supposed to make allowances for her.'

I turn away but Mum has me by the elbow.

'Paul . . .' she begins.

'Sheepsdogs,' Nonno says and taps his forehead. 'Sheepsdogs for Australian ghels.'

Mum narrows her eyes and looks at Nonno, then back at me.

'Go figure,' I say and walk out because I really just want to be alone.

16

'What's this all about, Paul?' Mum's followed me into the bedroom I share with Nonno.

'Why don't you get your *boyfriend* to investigate!' I yell, and push past Mum and stand leaning against the wall. 'He's a cop. He should be able to track down the information for you . . .'

'Paul!'

'*What*?' There's a throbbing pulse behind my eyes. It was there the night of Dad's funeral five years ago. I remember it so clearly – I had to get Nonno to cradle my head for hours because I thought it was going to explode. And Nonno just sat there beside my bed and rocked me to sleep, and when I woke up the next morning he was still there, beside my bed, cradling my head in his arms.

I'm looking at Mum and she's staring back at me, her eyes wide. She swallows. I watch the slow lump drop down her throat, and see her shoulders sag.

'Nothing, Paul,' she says. 'Nothing.'

I look at Nonno who's shuffled in behind Mum.

'What's *your* problem?' I spit at him.

Nonno doesn't answer right away. He fiddles with his walking-stick, rolling it slowly between the palms of his hands.

'I not like you be shame of me,' he says finally.

I shake my head and look down at my hands. 'I'm not shame of you,' I mumble. It's just that nothing's quite the same any more around the place: not Mum, not Zia Rita. Not me even. Not since Dad died.

I'd just like some space to myself. My own bedroom would be a good start. Somewhere apart from school that's a Nonno-free zone.

And I really want to be at the movies with Tracey. I mean, Mum can go to the movies with Constable Movies, so why can't I go with Tracey? Even if it is a Sunday night.

When I look up Nonno is sitting on his bed munching on his pistachio nuts and Mum's gone. Nonno offers me a handful but I'm not in the mood for them. Nonno shrugs and scratches his head.

'My papa catched me smoking the cigarettes hwuen I wos a boy, still not have hair under my nose,' he starts quietly. I prepare myself for another lecture on the distant past.

'But him not smacked me,' he continues. 'No. He sit me down in the stable with the donkey and the mule and he offer to me hims cigarettes. It was time of the soldiers be in my village. I remember clear like wos today.'

I know. I've heard him ranting on like this before.

'I remember we hiave to give to the soldiers the bread and cheese, maibe a chicken wot we killed, so they not burn down our house, not make trouble on our womens. You know, they wos with a *devil*. Devil him called Mussolini. Il Duce. But they wos not care about *us*!' Nonno spits and spittle runs down his chin. 'Cigarette wos cost much money because not much easy to find. But that day my papa made me to smoke every cigarette wot is in packet, one after nuther. Quick as I finish one, him lighted nuther. Smoke wos come out of my bum I wos hiave so many cigarettes!'

I look at Nonno. Just like him to go from one thing to another. I decide to humour him and nod. He seems pleased enough and goes on.

'I wos sick for *three* days after,' Nonno says with what sounds like anger, pressing a finger to the tip of his nose. 'For three days I wos lie in the bed and I wos cry and cough and call to my mama to help me. But my papa was shame of me because I wos take hims cigarettes behind hims back like I wos thief. Him said I wos thief in my own home! My papa wos angry like I never see before. My mama not allowed come help me, joust my papa come now and then make sure I not dead . . .'

Nonno's voice trails off yet again, like the thoughts have deserted him mid-sentence.

'Pity he didn't cure you of smoking then, eh,' I say.

But now Nonno doesn't seem to hear me. He narrows his eyes and taps his forehead lightly. He leans towards me, his voice softer than a moment before. He's slipped back into Italian. 'I remember it was the time when the soldiers executed my zio, my father's brother,' he says quietly. 'You know, they caught him stealing bread from the village priest's kitchen. It was when the priest's house was taken over by the commanders, and my zio, desperate for food for his children, thought the priests would have plenty to spare.'

Nonno pauses and blinks in my direction. 'The priests always seemed to have enough to eat. Even when our crops failed, the priests had more than enough to eat and drink. Maybe . . . maybe it was a miracle, who knows.' Nonno grins, but his eyes stay cold. 'My zio took a loaf of bread and one packet of cigarettes. He probably thought he could sell them somewhere and get money to buy food for us, for his family. Or maybe he wanted to smoke them himself. Maybe share them with my papa. I don't know. No one knows for sure. The dead don't talk.'

I'm looking directly at my nonno now. Because of all the stories he has ever told me, I have never heard this one before.

Nonno blinks and hoods his eyes. 'Why it is I joust forget all wrong tings. Better I forget long distance tings, not now tings,' he says more to himself than to me, I'm sure, because he's staring at his feet as he speaks.

Then he goes on . . .

'They shot my zio for those cigarettes, and left his bloodied body hanging in the piazza for two days,' Nonno continues in Italian again. 'They bound him up with rope from his own donkey's harness and they hung him upside down from the balcony outside the mayor's house. And then they made us all file past and look at him.'

Nonno looks straight at me and I shiver. 'I was a *boy*! But they made me walk past and look at what they had done to him! I remember my zia, his poor wife. She asked me to sing at his funeral, but I was still too sick from smoking all those cigarettes in the stable. My voice was too raw. I couldn't sing a note. I could barely whisper. So we buried my zio in silence.

'I was ashamed. My papa was ashamed.' Nonno pauses and blinks. 'It's a terrible thing to feel so ashamed before your family.'

Then Nonno is silent. His face is hard. Harder than I have ever seen it. 'My family was ashamed of *me*,' he adds. '*I* was ashamed of me.'

There's a huge lump in my throat. 'But it wasn't your fault,' I finally manage to squeeze out.

When Nonno doesn't answer I say, '*I'm* not ashamed of you.'

Nonno turns and shuffles out.

*

I'm still sitting here half an hour on. I feel numb. Nonno comes out with the most amazing things sometimes, and most times I just laugh them away. But I can't laugh now. This is different. It's like Nonno was trusting me with that story. That's what it feels like to me.

I'm scared. Nonno scares me. Not like 'spooky' scared. Not like 'I'm going to scream' scared. I mean 'sad' scared.

Paul Taranto, Formula 1 racing ace and English language guru, scared of a little old man who's losing his wits.

I collapse on my bed and stare up at the ceiling. I'd love to be with Tracey right now at the movies. Sure I would. Who wouldn't? Tracey Reynolds is hot hot *hot*.

I lie there on my bed and squeeze my eyes hard until little flashes of light explode before me. Until my eyes water.

I distract myself with thoughts about Tracey. I can almost feel Tracey's hand in mine, her thigh gently pressed against me as we sit side by side in the dark of the cinema, her warm breath close to my ear as she leans into my shoulder.

I think about reaching out and feeling the warmth of her skin, my fingertips probing the tops of her knees, my throat pumping as I try to swallow the pounding of my heart.

I take a deep breath and roll over onto my stomach. Sheeps! My nonno wants me to give Tracey's old man sheep as a kind of offering for his daughter's hand. I laugh. And then I hiccup. And then I feel the tears of anger welling up.

I know Zia Rita is wrong not to visit Nonno more than she does. I know Zia Rita is wrong for wanting Mum to put Nonno in a home. I know all that.

But just for a moment, just for a brief micro-second I find myself thinking that maybe Zia Rita is right after all. Maybe Nonno *is* becoming too much of a burden for Mum.

Maybe Nonno is becoming too much of a burden for *me*.

I can't ignore it any more. Nonno is going senile. Nonno is becoming unpredictable. Nonno is old. Nonno's got lost between two worlds.

These are Zia Rita's words. At least she's open about them. She doesn't try to hide them away like Mum does.

He's frail. He's confused. He's tired. Mum's words. Smokescreen words, Zia Rita calls them.

Mum and Zia argue about Nonno in front of him now, as though Nonno weren't there, or he can't understand. But he does.

Anyway, it's just not fair. Why do *I* have to be responsible for Nonno? Why do *I* have to sidestep my life because of Nonno? He had his chances. He had his time with Nonna Romina. I bet he didn't have *his* Nonno dragging him down. I bet if Dad were alive things would be different.

I stub my toe against Nonno's crate. My foot throbs but I kick at the crate again, and then again.

It's not fair! None of it. It's not even fair Nonno telling me about his zio being executed. It's not fair Nonno telling me about him being punished so harshly by his own father. He keeps dragging me back to his past. And then he reminds me of *my* past, of Dad. I don't need to know any more about any of it! I've got the future to worry about, not the friggin' past!

Then I think of Dad dying at work, with his mates around him doing nothing to stop it from happening.

And Nonno slipping away from me.

None of it's fair any more!

I grab some of Nonno's empty aftershave bottles from on top of the crate and hurl them out of the open window. I hear them shatter on the concrete, one by one.

17

It's like I'm being slapped in the face, listening to the sound of Nonno's precious bottles disintegrating outside the window of the bedroom we share. And then I can't help myself. I run through the house and into the garden.

There's a pain in my belly. I know what I've done but I don't want to believe it, so I bolt for the side of the house.

'What have you *done*, Paul! What have you done!'

It's Mum, and she's standing amongst the broken glass, one hand over her mouth.

Nonno is beside her. He's staring at the mess in silence.

'What have you done, Paul?' Mum says again. Not really a question.

When I try to say I'm sorry, that I don't know why I've done what I've done, Nonno refuses to say anything to me. He just blinks and rocks slowly back and forth, using his walking-stick for support. Once she gets over her shock, Mum orders me to clean up the mess. I don't have to be told twice, especially because Nonno just stands there staring into the scattered fragments of glass.

'Teresa, maibe you friend the policeman he can come talk to Paul. Him can tell Paul dat is not good ting to destroy wot is not yours,' Nonno finally says when I've finished sweeping away the glass.

'I don't think Paul would listen to anything any male friend of mine might have to say,' Mum answers in a voice Lady Fang might use on me as a last resort before she sends me out of the room.

I'm unravelling the garden hose because Mum wants me to get rid of every last tiny bit of broken glass, and I can feel Mum's eyes on me.

She's right. Constable Movies can tell me all he wants about respecting other people's stuff. I don't have to listen to him. Not apart from the fact that he's a cop. He's not my dad. Never will be. No one ever will be.

Not even Nonno.

Better Nonno than some other bloke, though. At least Nonno is family. At least Nonno has always been here. He's not some blow-in interested in my mum. Mum is safe with Nonno. I'm safe with Nonno.

That's another reason why I maybe don't want Nonno to be put away in a home, or a retirement village.

Nonno keeps Mum busy. Too busy, until recently at least, to get on with her own life. Having Nonno around stops Mum getting serious about . . . well, about guys and stuff.

Maybe that's not completely true. Even if Mum did get involved with someone, I still wouldn't want Nonno taken away.

'I didn't mean to smash your bottles,' I whisper to Nonno when I'm done rolling away the hose. 'I lost my marbles.'

'Another time when I was young man, I lost my papa's goats,' Nonno says in his dialect without looking at me.

'Yeah, right,' I say and shake my head. That's really all I need now, another of Nonno's boyhood stories. I'm still trying to register the one about the execution.

'I wos look after goats evri dai,' Nonno continues in English. 'Wos my job. But I hate it so much. I wos alone all the day. Just me and the goats. And one dai I see a ghel wot I like and I tink myself the goats can look after self while me go talk to dis ghel. In those dais not easy for boy talk wit ghel, evrihuan always see. I tink to myself good time now for me to joust say hello dis ghel.'

Nonno wipes at an eye with the tip of his finger, but still he won't look at me.

'I wos young, hiave plenty strength,' he continues. 'I check see goats him okay, and then me go to the ghel. She veri shy of me, so for long time joust me talk talk talk. After time she talk too and soon we talk so much dat time fly away. When I go back my goats gone!' Nonno pushes the air with a closed fist. 'I call and call, and walk and walk but not can find goats. Because I know my papa him be veri angry with me I not go home dat night. Instead I go hide in haystack of neighbour farm . . .'

Nonno's voice trails off into silence. I see him frown. He taps his walking-stick on the ground.

'You had no right to break my bottles,' he says in his Italian dialect, slowly so that I can understand. 'I didn't do anything to you, Paolo.' Nonno pauses, draws a deep breath that seems to take ages to fill his lungs, then adds in English, 'Sometime you need stop and tink what you do before you do it, Paul.'

Nonno finally looks at me. The skin around his eyes and mouth is loose, folded in creases I've never really noticed before. He looks sadder than I've seen him in a long time, maybe even since the day of Dad's funeral. He cried a lot that day, my nonno, like he'd lost his own son. Like he'd lost his zio all over again.

I want to say something but by the time I try to work out exactly what, Nonno is talking in Italian again.

'When I lost the goats I was so scared to go back home that I stayed away until, after two days, hunger drove me home. By then my poor mama was beside herself with fear for my well-being, and my papa was frantic with worry because he knew in his heart why I hadn't gone straight home to tell him what had happened.' Nonno chews silently for a few moments.

'But maybe that is the past, Paolo,' he says with a nod. 'Like my bottles. The past. We have to let it go sometime. Sweep it away. It's not good to hang onto the past for too long, Paolo. Not good.'

I'm trying to organise my brain around what he's saying. 'Did you ever find the goats?' I ask.

'The goats? Yes, we find them,' Nonno grins. 'On hooks in another paesano's farm.'

He must recognise my look of astonishment because Nonno adds, 'It's difficult to recognise a goat as yours once he's been skinned and gutted. But some things you just know, Paolo. Some things you just know.'

'Well, next time I have any goats to look after I'll make sure I don't go off to chat up a girl,' I say through clenched teeth. I don't know if I want to be the keeper of his stories.

'Paolo,' Nonno snaps and I see his eyes narrow. Then more softly he adds, 'Paolo, I want show you something.'

Nonno hobbles off, leaving me to follow him back into the house, down the hallway and back to our bedroom. I go along. It's the least I can do after what I did to his collection of aftershave bottles.

'Close it the door,' he commands and I give the door a nudge with my foot. It clicks shut.

I go to speak but Nonno raises a finger to his lips and nods for me to sit on my bed. Then, as I watch, he fumbles about in his waistcoat pocket for a few moments, finally pulling out a key. It's the same key he showed me before – the one he called his magic key. He uses it now to unlock the crate marked *Mildura Oranges – Fresh and Delicious. R. Trotter & Sons*. But not before he has carefully folded the doily where all his precious aftershave bottles have rested for as many years as I can remember.

I wince at the thought of all those broken bottles now. All those bottles, like the one he'd shown me the other night, the one he'd said I had given him. All those bottles attaching my nonno to some other time, and some other person.

All those bottles did so much more than stop Nonno smelling like a goat.

Nonno has his back to me as he works kneeling on the floor, but I see his shoulders rise and fall.

'You haven't got a goat locked away in there, have you, Nonno?' I say finally because I can't stand the silence between us, and because I'm feeling queasy all of a sudden. It's like Nonno is about to reveal something else to me that I may not want to know.

All these years we've shared the bedroom, Nonno has never ever opened that crate while I've been around. Never.

But Nonno doesn't answer.

I swallow and lick my lips. They're drying out as I sit there on the edge of my bed.

I can't help but think again that perhaps Zia Rita is right. Perhaps poor Nonno needs to be somewhere where he can get professional help. I think maybe that he's going to pull out something hideous from that crate. Why else does he want the door shut, and why else would he keep an orange crate padlocked?

That crate didn't come out from Italy with him. I've always known that. And Nonno must know that I know that. The crate comes from Mildura in north-western Victoria. But he's always insisted that the crate came out with him on the ship from Naples all those years ago, before even I was born.

The lid squeaks open and I try to sneak a peek over Nonno's shoulder. But he gives me a stern stare and I drop my gaze to the floor.

I think every past thought I've ever had about the contents of Nonno's crate. More empty aftershave bottles? Personal papers revealing that he is actually an illegal immigrant? Copies of bank statements documenting Nonno's hidden fortunes? Or maybe rolls and rolls of banknotes bound up with rubber bands and covered after all these years in a fine layer of dust . . .

Or maybe a cache of weapons from a past secret life? Or newspaper articles talking about Nonno's exploits as a crime fighter? Or a mobster. The Don, with his own army of would-be thugs and try-hards at his disposal, hanging off his every word, ready to do his bidding without hesitation. If he'd been old enough back then, The Don would have sent those fascists packing, I bet!

Wouldn't Dan be impressed! Kiss my ring!

Nonno turns to face me. With a short stab of his finger he asks me to join him.

I get down on my knees next to Nonno and look into his crate. Nope. No banknotes or submachine guns. Instead there's a small box, its lid vaulted and heavily carved with figures of sheep and cattle and goats. It rests on a cushion made from what appears to be part of an old mattress. Maybe the box is Nonno's handiwork? I wonder, and know the answer even as the question occurs to me. Nonno used to be great with his hands. Mum's told a thousand stories about how Nonno would knock together all sorts of wooden furniture and toys for them when she and Zia Rita were little girls. How he would build odds and ends for Nonna Romina.

Nonno reaches past me and slips a second much smaller key into a tiny lock on the latch of the small box. He lifts the lid.

The inside is amazing. It's all padded with stuff that looks like white silk, folded and folded into a kind of repeated pillow effect. There is not a trace of mildew or dust. It's spotless.

And right in the middle of it all, nestled in the bottom, there's something shiny with a blue and red ribbon attached.

I reach in to touch it. It looks like a medal. But Nonno's hand slaps mine away.

'Only when I am gone!' Nonno says in his Italian dialect and smiles at me when I turn a hard look on him. 'Then it is yours, Paolo. Today I just let you look at it.'

'What is it?' I ask.

'What it is?' Nonno says and I see him stare at the medal as though searching for something written on it. 'It is a reminder that even a goatherd could have been more than he is, Paolo. My music, Paolo. My singing. I was *free* with my music! My music made me so much more than a goatherd, Paolo. So much more,' Nonno tells me sadly. Then he carefully turns the medal over and I see the inscription. Before I can begin to read it for myself, Nonno reads it to me, in precise Italian.

'Medal of Distinction. Campagna. Finalist. Music Section. 1940.'

Nonno's voice is strange to my ears. I've only ever really heard him speak his village dialect, not the same formal Italian I recognise from classes at school.

'This was presented to me same year my zio was killed,' Nonno explains. 'Mussolini and his blackshirts – they had told teachers and civic leaders the country over to find the most talented young people in the arts. They wanted to show the rest of the world just how progressive the Italian government was. How talented were its people. And *I* . . .' Nonno sighs, as though the memory is too heavy to bear. '*I* was selected as the most outstanding young singer of our region. I had a voice as clear as a bell. Perfect pitch and tone. I was twelve years old.'

Nonno narrows his eyes and frowns slightly.

'And?' I prompt.

'The war,' he says simply. 'The war, and then nothing. I had it all planned out, Paolo. As well as a goatherd can, of course. With the help of the village priest. And the local committee. It was set up to prepare finalists from our region. We were to travel to Napoli for the event! I rehearsed my song over and over until I knew it so well it might have been woven into me.'

Nonno pauses. His fingers caress the medal. His lips turn up in a sad smile. 'And then it was over. All promises torn apart.' He blinks. 'The only time I went to Napoli was when I left Italy for good.'

Then Nonno waves a hand around. 'But is all the past. Must let go the past. Must let it die,' he says, lapsing back into his dialect. He wipes at something that might be a tear in the corner of one eye.

'You never got to perform that song?' I ask as Nonno slaps shut the box. 'You didn't even get to sing at your uncle's funeral, did you?'

'In the years after the war I sang to my goats, yes, many times,' Nonno continues. 'But my goats were more interested in thistles than arias.' He swallows and blinks slowly, tears in the corners of his eyes. 'After they killed my zio I never wanted to sing again. Too much pain here,' he adds and touches first his chest, then mine, with an open palm.

I look at Nonno. Really look at him, for the first time.

'Is that why you don't ever want to go back to Monte Sereno?' I say in a voice that scratches at the back of my throat. 'Is that why, when . . . is that why you don't want to be back in Italy with Nonna Romina?'

Nonno sighs and there is a sad, sad faraway look in his eyes. I feel Nonno's sadness, and my own, and we sit there on the floor of our bedroom and I watch him rock gently back and forth.

I want to keep Nonno with me – with us – for as long as I can now. But deep down I know that already I'm losing him. The Don is not what he used to be, even a few months ago. And all the stories. All the memories Nonno is sharing with me. He is passing them on, before they are lost, even to him.

One thing for sure, I'll never let Zia Rita, or Mum for that matter, take Nonno away.

18

She has been toying with the idea for months, Zia Rita announces over the phone to Mum, and now she's decided. She's moving right away. To Sydney.

'"I'm just not cut out for being a *housemaid* to Dad, sorry."' Mum is mimicking Zia's voice really well.

'"But you had him for just one night, Rita." That's what I told her! One night!' Mum tells me.

Mum does a pretty good imitation of her sister, cheesy Barbie smile and all. The artistic flourish must run in the family.

'"Yeah, well, some things don't take a lifetime to work out, you know." That's how she answered me! Can you believe it?' Mum continues.

Nonno is sitting at the kitchen table, one arm resting on it, the other holding his walking-stick at full stretch.

I reckon he's not too pleased about Zia Rita taking

off for Sydney. I know I'm right because at the mention of the word 'Sydney' Nonno flinches.

'But hey, what difference does it make where your zia is, right, Paul?' says Mum. 'It's not like she visits a whole lot. It's not as though she ever just drops by to take her dad for a walk or shopping. Maybe even take dad out for coffee. I don't know what, anything . . .' Mum is talking down into the ironing board, a sure sign that she's upset.

'And you, Paul,' she says, suddenly looking right at me. 'Don't think you can get away with what you did to your nonno's bottles. Right now, I'm in the mood to send you to that boarding school in Monte Sereno. Maybe some time away from Dan and your go-carts will make you realise just how unimpressed I am with your behaviour lately.'

I look back at Mum with a steady gaze. She's not the only one not impressed with my behaviour. I'm not too impressed with me, either.

'Detentions, smashing bottles . . . leaving your nonno like you did. You try me sometimes, Paul. You really try me.'

'More than Zia Rita?' I say before I can stop myself. I grimace. 'Sorry, Mum.'

I look at Nonno again. He's grinning at me. We exchange a quick conspiratorial smile and I wonder if Mum knows anything of what The Don has shared with me.

I sidle up to Mum and take a quick breath. I need to know.

'Has Nonno ever talked to you about the war?' I ask. 'I mean, has Nonno ever mentioned . . .' I stop and look back at Nonno.

Nonno is shaking his head. 'Wot for Sidiney?' he says in a huff. 'Wot them got there dat is not here?'

I look at Mum. We both know what Sydney hasn't got that so appeals to Zia Rita. All three of us know, but I reckon Mum isn't ready to admit yet that Nonno has it all figured out as well. I guess Mum can't cope with the thought of Nonno knowing that one of his own daughters could walk out on him.

I turn back to Mum. I slip an arm around her waist. Mum looks at me. I haven't done that for such a long time she must think I want something.

'Nonno had it pretty hard during the war, eh,' I say. 'Has Nonno ever like, you know, talked to you about that time in his life?'

Mum stops pressing the iron into one of her T-shirts and fixes me with a stare. I have my answer. It's there on Mum's face.

'It's a long time ago,' Mum whispers quickly.

'But he remembers it so clearly!' I tell Mum. 'It's like it happened yesterday.'

I see Mum hesitate. She swallows and casts a glance at Nonno. 'What's he told you? He's told you about his zio?' she asks.

I nod. Mum puts the iron down and runs her hand around my face. 'He was a young man then, no older than you probably,' she says softly. 'There are some things no one should have to live with, Paul. When your zia Rita and I were little girls, and your nonno would get angry at the smallest thing, your nonna Romina used to tell us not to forget what he'd been through. I used to think it was your nonna making excuses for him, but I've changed my mind since then.'

Mum's eyes have gone all fuzzy. She wipes at them quickly. 'People of your nonno's generation, Paul, so many of them suffered in ways you and I cannot possibly understand,' she adds finally.

I look at Mum for a long time. I plant a kiss on her cheek. We'll be okay, the three of us, I realise at that moment. Even with Zia Rita taking off for Sydney. Mum, Nonno and me, we're going to be okay.

I don't say anything though. I give Nonno a wink instead. He slips me a lopsided grin. I try to high-five Nonno but he just looks at my hand hanging in mid-air and waves his spoon about. Milk flies everywhere.

'She never strong enough,' Nonno manages between a mouthful of pasta dura bread he has had soaking in warm milk for the past five minutes. He scoops the soggy bread up with his spoon and the milk dribbles down his chin.

'Not like Mum, eh, Nonno?' I grin.

'Yes, you mama much more stronger than him sister,'

Nonno replies. 'She not need go Sidiney like Rita. You mama like stay here wit us. Special now she got a boyfriend wot is a pig.'

'Dad!' Mum exclaims.

Nonno frowns innocently. 'In my village pig is veri good!' he adds. 'Is like money. More pigs you got, more wealthy you is. But . . . must be *fat*. Not fat, not good.'

I laugh. Things are different now. Maybe it was Nonno's story about his uncle, about his voice. The medal even. Maybe it was thinking about Dad. Or maybe it's just that it's Monday morning and I'm about to see Tracey Reynolds again. Either way, it's been a long weekend!

But what I do know for certain is that something *has* changed in the last two days. I feel like all the thick gunk that has been inside me these past five years is spewing out and spreading at my feet. I feel like I'm breathing a whole lot of clean fresh air for a change.

'Mum, you having . . .' I think about what I'm going to say a sec because I don't want to sound like a push-over. 'You thinking of having Constable Movies over for a dinner of one of your famous lasagne dishes?'

I'm not looking at Mum but I know she's stopped dead in her tracks and is probably staring at me again.

'Dan reckons you're still pretty okay. For a mum,' I add because Mum likes a compliment, even if it is from Dan Declan. Sort of.

'I beg your pardon?' Mum snorts.

I pull a face, look at Nonno, but he's slurping the last of his milk and probably hasn't heard a word.

'I just meant that . . .' I swallow. 'I didn't mean it to sound like . . .' Go on, say it. *Say it*!

This is heaps harder than I thought it would be.

Formula 1 racing ace, English language guru, Paul 'The Don' Taranto, shames mother to early death. Speculation rife that The Don may now retire his rogue tongue to a museum for curiosities in southern Queensland.

Mum is looking at Nonno. I can see she's embarrassed that Nonno's overhearing all of this.

I swallow again. 'I just mean that I know, I guess, that I have to be okay about you and . . .' I begin.

'Wayne?'

I nod. 'Yeah, *Wayne*.' The name still sticks a bit, though.

Nonno shuffles in his chair. 'Wine? Okay! Give to me some wine!' he calls.

Mum and I ignore him.

'He's a *friend*, Paul, that's all.' Mum says.

I hear Mum's words like they're from a long way off.

'I'm allowed to have a friend, aren't I, Paul?' It's not really a question. It's one of those Lady Fang type comments that just seem to be questions: late again, are we, Mr Taranto? Have an exception from PE today, Mr Taranto, do you? You'd like me to send you to the principal, Mr Taranto?

'I'm still relatively young, Paul. I can't just roll up in a ball and die. Just because I enjoy the company of a man other than your dad now that he's gone, that doesn't mean I don't still miss your dad, Paul. I do. I miss him every day. In so many ways.'

I'm listening to Mum but watching Nonno. He's finished his pasta dura and his hands are fiddling with thin air.

I look down at the floor, at the tiles Mum keeps so shiny clean you could eat off them.

I see Mum's shadow shift on the table. She gets to her feet and pushes her chair in.

'Every time I look at you, Paul, I'm reminded of your dad and why I loved . . . why I love him so much. Nothing and no one will ever replace him, Paul. Not for me, and I know, not for you. Especially not for you. And that's how it should be. People can't just be replaced that easily, Paul.'

Mum is standing now about an arm's length away. I can just see her bare feet. She has nice toes, my mum. Neat and tidy, with nails she keeps painted in pale red.

'I'd never even think about replacing your dad, Paul. I'd never do anything to make you think that,' she says. 'But if I have, I'm sorry. I really am.'

The red toes shift. Mum is getting ready to give me one of her hugs. I can feel it.

And that's when Nonno snorts really loudly.

So loudly that Mum and I look up at him together.

'I wos choke,' Nonno grins and points to his throat. 'The milk, him got stuck!'

Mum touches me lightly on the elbow.

'Thanks for what you said,' she whispers, 'about Wayne. I appreciate it. But he *is* just a friend.'

I swallow again, but can't say anything back.

All I know for certain is that Mum deserves a little breathing space of her own. Ever since Dad died she's been crowded in by me and Nonno, and Zia Rita too, in her own selfish way. Maybe I've just been scared of losing her. Like we did Dad. It's like, you can't just rein someone in because you're scared they might go away. Dad didn't go by choice. I know that.

Nonno says he won't ever leave his home here with us if he has his way. I reckon Nonno's pretty safe on that score, especially with Zia Rita taking off to Sydney. Zia Rita can try to run away I guess, but she can't really hide. One day she'll be back. You can never escape family. Not completely.

I look at Nonno. Just like you can't escape the past, no matter what tricks your mind tries to pull on you.

'Yo, Taranto, you ready to *roll*?' Dan is at our back door, right on time, like every Monday morning before school. I never thought I'd think it, but seeing Dan standing there now I almost wish I had the guts to plant a big kiss on both his cheeks, the way Italian men like my nonno do when they're really rapt to see a mate. And I'm rapt to see Dan right now, really stoked.

'Thanks for the note,' I say as we rush out the back door, but really I'm thanking him for rescuing me back there just now. I don't know what else Mum probably wanted to say to me, or what else I might have said to her. Telling her it was okay to invite Constable Movies over for lasagne is more than enough for the time being. Besides, I've had enough gushy feelings for one morning. Unless of course Tracey Reynolds wants to . . .

'So, you had a good time at Tracey's place?' Dan asks and arches his eyebrows.

'It was okay.' Better to be non-committal.

'Not what I heard, mate.'

I stop and let Dan get a few paces ahead. Even from the back he has a face only a mother could love.

'Oh? What have you heard?' I ask with as much indifference as I can.

Dan stops and I see his shoulders square. He looks back at me and winks. 'Bahmir reckons you had one tiny sip of whisky and almost choked to death. He reckons you were sloshed on the fumes alone and left before anything could get going between you and Tracey . . .'

'Bahmir needs his brains drained,' I snap. 'He spends too much time with Magda and he's gone soft in the head.'

I walk on because this is a stupid conversation.

'But you didn't get to *kiss* Tracey, did you?' Dan sneers. 'I mean, you had a few sniffs of the whisky and passed out! Until Tracey told you it was time you went home.'

I look at Dan and realise that I don't actually remember what happened at Tracey's. Not clearly, anyway. The clearest thought in my mind from Saturday evening was getting back to Zia Rita's and finding that Nonno had done a runner.

Maybe I didn't get to pash with Tracey Reynolds after all.

Maybe even my mum's got a more exciting love-life than I have!

Suddenly I'm not so hot on seeing Tracey Reynolds this morning. Not in a group situation, anyway. Not until I can suss out from her what did or didn't happen between us.

I just might be in the running here for the shortest romantic fling in the history of mankind. The world, even. Good one.

Formula 1 racing ace, English language guru, and part-time Nonno-finder, Paul 'The Don' Taranto, lucks out with beautiful Tracey Reynolds. Blink-and-you-missed-it romance a world record.

19

Lady Fang ignores me right through homeroom, but just as she's ready to dismiss us to our first class I trap her at her desk.

'My zia said to tell you she's got a heap more second-hand books you might want to buy real cheap, Miss Wildermere,' I smile.

Lady Fang coughs into her hand and eyeballs the back of the room.

'Thank you,' she whispers, but I can tell she's not really impressed about me mentioning the garage sale.

Dan, who is right at my elbow, smirks. I've told him all about Lady Fang buying the books on Saturday.

'I'll write down the titles of the books if you want, Miss,' I say cheerfully. 'My zia reckons you were one of our best customers and . . .'

But I don't get to finish. Lady Fang snaps her head back in my direction, her lips part and she shows me the tips of her teeth.

'I've got quite enough reading material for the moment, thank you just the same,' she hisses. I'm about to say something witty about the bargains people find at garage sales when Lady Fang adds, 'However, I *am* looking forward to reading your assignment on oral stories, Paul.'

Oral stories assignment? What oral stories assignment?

Lady Fang must see the question, *What oral stories assignment?* written across my forehead, because she raises both eyebrows and looks down her nose at me.

Dan suddenly decides he has to get to first period. But Lady Fang bails him up with, 'There's never smoke without fire,' which I guess is supposed to mean something deep. But it gets translated by Lady Fang as 'You two are a pair, and again, what one fails to hand in, the other likewise.'

I look at Dan. The question, *What oral stories assignment?* bores into his head.

'I gather from the look of utter incredulity on both your faces that neither of you realises what today is,' Lady Fang announces.

If she spoke English like normal people I might be able to give her an answer. As it is, Lady Fang has to fill me in, and Dan too.

'Several weeks ago I set the class a research task. It was based on our discussions of traditions. Of societies passing down their stories orally from one generation to the next,' she says matter-of-factly. I can see she is enjoying explaining all this because Lady Fang is actually smiling. Smirking is probably closer.

'The work is due in today. *Now*, in fact,' she continues. She points at a pile of papers on her desk. 'But of course you two were too busy down the back there to hear me ask for them.'

She's right there. I was busy down the back of the room, waiting for a break in the girl-chat to get a word in with Tracey about the weekend. As it was, Tracey was in a deep-and-meaningful with Magda so I didn't get a chance. I'm going to try again at recess.

Lady Fang pulls herself up to her full height, which is about the height of a fully grown silverback gorilla, only heaps less attractive.

'No assignment, no mark.' Lady Fang smiles.

'But Miss . . .' starts Dan and stops when Lady Fang turns the evil eye on him. Dan scratches at his face and looks at me.

I shrug. Dan rolls his eyes. He needs to fail another English assignment the way I need another detention.

Lady Fang collects her books, licks her bottom lip and turns to walk out.

I've been so caught up with The Don and the problems about Zia Rita that I've completely forgotten the assignment. I haven't done any more on it since Nonno filled in the blanks on the short-answer questionnaire. And drooling over Tracey Reynolds hasn't helped. And not having the Internet at home.

I'm about to tell Lady Fang to give me a fair break. I'm about to tell her about my lousy weekend, when I have a brainwave.

'I bet everyone's written really detailed stuff about this oral stories business, eh, Miss?' I say slowly.

Lady Fang stops. I see her neck stiffen. I nudge Dan to keep silent and I take a quick breath.

'I bet everyone's handed in pages and pages of notes and stuff about oral history and how people sat around campfires and stuff and told stories long into the night.' I'm talking about two words behind my thoughts, making it up as I go. 'Looks like you've got heaps of reading to do about oral stories, Miss.'

Dan is pinching me, a sure sign he wants me to shut up. I give him a gentle shove. I get up and circle Lady Fang until I'm blocking her exit.

'Sort of defeats the purpose, doesn't it, Miss? To write down on paper all that stuff about oral stories,' I say. 'Me and Dan have actually done a really top combined assignment . . .' I look past Lady Fang. Dan is pummelling his forehead with his fists. I ignore him. 'I mean, it's a good idea to write the stories themselves down so they won't be forgotten and all, but . . .'

I pause for dramatic effect. I learnt all about that in Year 9 drama last year.

Lady Fang shuffles so that she can look at both me and Dan, but I move in front of her again so that she has to look at me, since I'm doing all the talking. I go on . . .

'You see, me and Dan decided we'd go one step further, Miss,' I explain, calculating my words carefully because I'm barely aware of exactly what it is I've sort of conjured up out of nothing. 'You just caught us by surprise, that's all. We've got a great assignment, really we have, a combined effort.' I lower my eyes to the floor but I can sense Lady Fang's startled face.

'You won't be sorry, Miss. Period 4 today, in English class. Promise.'

I look hard at Dan. It takes me a few moments but he finally gets the hint. 'Top assignment, really,' he says to Lady Fang, and I almost want to whack him on the side of the head.

I watch Lady Fang grinding her teeth. She's got her eyes narrowed and looks from me to Dan and back again. The second bell for the start of the first period sounds. I swallow.

'Top assignment, you say?' she says slowly. 'It better be.' And she strides out.

'That was close,' I announce.

'Top assignment!' drawls Dan. 'I've got mine in my bag in my locker! Why'd you get me involved in this *bulldust*, Taranto? All I wanted to do was ask if I could go get it . . . Well, the bit I've done anyway . . .'

I drop an arm around Dan's shoulders. 'When did you actually do your assignment, Declan?' I ask.

'Last night.'

'You did a couple of weeks work in one night,' I grin. 'Must be a ripper assignment.'

Dan shrugs. 'Well, it's a whole lot better than *nothin'* at all!'

'Maybe. Maybe not. Depends.'

'You talking crap again, Taranto?'

I shake my head. 'Nah, don't reckon I am,' I smile. 'Trust me on this one, Danny Boy!'

'Yeah, right!' Dan pulls himself free and shakes his head. 'And don't call me Danny Boy!' he snaps.

'Sure thing.' I slap Dan on the back. 'Look, just cover for me in PE, willya,' I tell him and head for the corridor.

'We've got indoor cricket first up!' I hear Dan call after me.

'Good! Tell Mr Symonds I'm in sick bay.'

'With *what*?'

'Athlete's foot!' I call back and crash through the doors out into the Quad.

The wall behind the girls' toilet block is the lowest and the easiest one to get over without being spotted, so I head for it. There's a lane that leads out to the local park, and from there it's a short sprint home.

I don't know where my ideas come from sometimes. It's like they pop into my head out of nowhere. I'm probably an undiscovered genius.

I'm an undiscovered genius with a good ear for

other people's voices. Hear a voice once and that's it. I can usually pick it in one when I hear it again.

Tracey Reynolds's voice makes a sound like dripping honey. So I nail her voice instantly and pull up short of the wall.

It's not the polite thing to do, I know. To listen in on other people's conversations. But she could be talking about me and Saturday and how much she loves Don Paul and his 'fast toy'.

'So I ring him, right.' I hear her dulcet tones. I learnt that word in music class. It means soft and inviting. 'I ring the big Don Paul at home and he gives me this *suck* story about not being able to go out with me! Because . . . get this . . . he had to stay home and look after his grandfather. Like, give me a break! I mean, my wrinkly gran would never expect me to stay home and hold her bloody hand if she was sick. No way.'

'*Your* grandmother doesn't live with you, Tracey. She lives in Queensland or somewhere.'

'Brisbane, actually,' Tracey corrects Magda. 'One of those old people's homethingies.'

Toilet walls are cold. I know because I'm pressing my cheek against one so's I can hear more.

'But that's not the best part.' Tracey again. She stops suddenly and I press myself right up against the wall. 'Hold my fag a sec, Mags.'

There's silence. Then someone blows her nose.

'Best part is,' Tracey continues after a moment.

'Best part is that Paul's grandfather got on the phone and started talking down the line at me in this gibberish English only another ethnic could understand ... Sorry Mags, no offence ... But it was bizarre, right. He calls me tractor or trackydak or something like that ... can't even get my name right ...'

Tracey splutters, coughs, then adds, 'The old guy said something about getting me *sheep*. What's that supposed to mean, you reckon?'

Magda laughs and then Tracey laughs with her.

'Should have heard the old fella. "You like Paul, yes?"' Tracey's voice is bare. Sharp as a knife. 'Der, like I'm going to *marry* him, right. As if. I mean, I thought the guy was cool, you know, on account of the go-carts and his looks. And Bahmir and Dan talking together about how Paul's grandfather is some kind of big-shot Don who nicks cars. Someone even the cops are scared of. I mean, I figured Paul was going to be like those silent but deadly guys in those movies about New York and stuff. How wrong was I! Turns out Don Paul likes to play house-nurse to some old fart. I mean, *pl-ee-se!*'

More laughter, then Tracey again. 'Did you see him try to scull his drinks at my place on Saturday? I was shocked, you know. There I was, thinking this guy's hot for a good time, and he winds up coughing up most of my old man's grog all over himself! And I thought maybe Taranto was different to the other dorky try-hards in this place ...'

If I press a little harder I reckon I'll go through the wall, which probably wouldn't be a bad thing given as I feel like knocking Tracey Reynolds out right at this moment. I swallow again and it's like there's a sharp razor going down my throat. But I can't just walk away.

'Don Paul phoned me on Saturday night, my sister reckons,' Tracey continues. 'Probably wanted me to babysit his grandfather with him.'

'Yeah. You could have helped rinse out the grand-father's falsies!' Magda splutters.

'Sure thing, and then we could have spent the rest of the night teaching the old codger how to say my name properly!' Tracey's laugh explodes and I step away from the wall and walk away. Right into the girls' toilets.

I don't give Tracey or Magda time to be shocked to see me.

I'm pointing at Tracey. 'You don't know the first thing about my nonno,' I say as calmly as I can. 'You don't have a *clue* about what sort of bloke he really is.'

I see Tracey's eyes bulge. Suddenly she doesn't seem so drop-dead gorgeous any more. She backs away like I've just shoved her. Magda is speechless, too.

'You know, I really feel sorry for your grandmother in Brisbane, Tracey,' I continue, not even pausing for a breath. 'Imagine having someone like *you* talking about her like she's a piece of old furniture you've chucked in a back room somewhere. At least my nonno won't ever be left alone in some home somewhere.'

I see Tracey flinch and I fix my gaze on her. 'I'm not ashamed of *my* nonno. In fact, I reckon he's a great bloke. Heaps better than some people I know. Heaps . . .'

I can't go on. I walk out. My heart's pounding in my head. Tracey and Magda are going to tell everyone about what I just did. I know they will. But I don't care any more. I just don't care.

20

I can hardly walk. My insides feel like jelly. I can't *believe* what I've just done.

Nonno and his blasted sheep. Seems like everything I ever do he's involved in somewhere. If it's not by defacing my English homework, then it's by making me look like a major loser with Tracey.

And now Tracey thinks Nonno called her Tractor! Like I come from a family where people can't even speak simple English! Oh God!

If it wasn't for Nonno I probably could have gone to the movies with Tracey last night and she would have been telling Magda how cool I was, instead of making me out to be the king of the weird people. If it wasn't for Nonno living with us there would have been a very different conversation on the phone last night. Sure Tracey, I'd love to tag along to the movies, I would have said. What time and where? No, I don't have a curfew. No, there's no one here I have to babysit. Sure we can stay out and hit the arcades after-wards, if that's what you'd like to do.

Instead I said I'd be there in spirit! Instead Nonno gets on the phone and tells Tracey he's been looking for sheep for her. Instead Nonno asks *Tratcy* if she likes me!

When I'm a famous and fabulously rich Formula 1 racing ace I'm going to buy a house as far away from here as I can find. One of those sprawling estates that have their own golf course and zoo and Olympic-size swimming pool and two-metre-high walls enclosing it to keep undesirables out.

And I'm going to live in it alone.

Just me.

Paul 'The Don' Taranto, alone. Except for the people I invite to stay over when I want company. And Dan can be my manager. He can hire Bahmir to be my bodyguard and Bahmir can keep the hordes of fans at bay. And he can tell Tracey Reynolds that no she can't have an audience with me. She had her chance in Year 10 and blew it. And anyway, I'm not into *shallow, super-ficial chicks* like her any more.

And Mum can move in with Constable Movies and they can build a Nonno-flat at the back of *their* place, somewhere far away from my place where Nonno can mumble on the phone to whoever he wants to, so long as he doesn't involve *me*.

That's what I'm going to do when I'm a famous and fabulously rich Formula 1 racing ace. And no one is going to stop me. Not even Dad. Especially not Dad. Because Dad is dead.

I stop and lean against someone's back fence.

It's been five years since Dad died. Suddenly I want him here again. Suddenly I just want to hug Dad and ask him if life is always this complicated or if it gets easier the older you get.

I bite my lip and take a deep breath. It's like when Nonno told me about his medal, about his dreams – it's like a hole that can't be plugged.

Tracey Reynolds thinks I'm a loser on account of me having to look after Nonno. *Bullshit*! Tracey has it wrong. She has *no* idea about The Dons. None whatsoever.

Nor does Zia Rita.

Zia Rita is terrified of Nonno. I saw it when I watched her during the garage sale. I saw it in the way she avoided making eye contact with Nonno the entire time. I saw it when she asked Nonno to play some of those old traditional tunes on his piano accordion. The only tunes he can *still* remember by heart. He told me he learnt them by ear, as a young boy sitting on his own dad's knee.

That's why Zia Rita has to move to Sydney. Nonno scares her. Not 'spooky' scares her, 'heartbreak' scares her.

It's the fear of what is happening to Nonno. If Nonno is put in a home Zia Rita can pretend like he's already dead. If Nonno is put in a home, Zia Rita won't have to pretend that Mum and me *understand* why she doesn't visit.

Out of sight, out of mind.

It's hit me now how sad Zia Rita must be. Deep down, she can't bring herself to face what is happening to Nonno.

Zia Rita *has* to move to Sydney. She has to, because she knows Mum will never let Nonno go into a home, not while she can still care for him.

I draw a breath, shut my eyes and keep walking. The cool morning air on my bare arms makes my skin tingle and goosebumps stand out.

Now it's clear to me. I know what I have to do, and it's not what I was going to do a few minutes earlier.

When I ran out of school I had a great idea. I'd break open Nonno's crate and borrow his medal. I was going to take the medal to school and show it to Lady Fang and the class during English and tell them that *this* was my oral histories assignment, my talking about Nonno's past, about how he had once been chosen to represent his region as a singer.

I have flashes of brilliance like that sometimes. I saw myself standing at the front of the class and talking about Nonno's medal and how it was a sort of link to oral stories. I was going to make something up about oral stories and objects and how you can remember stories better if you have an object to help trigger the main points of the story. Like the date and the inscription on the back of the medal could trigger different parts of Nonno's story.

I'd make it up as I went.

But I can't do that now.

Nonno deserves better than that.

The Don didn't deserve to have his aftershave bottles smashed. He didn't deserve to have me or Zia Rita joke about slapping a 'For Sale' sign on his forehead. He didn't deserve to see his zio shot when he was only twelve years old.

Tracey doesn't understand that. Zia Rita doesn't understand it, either.

Mum does though. And Dad, too, if he'd still been alive.

I remember something Lady Fang talked about in English class. About tradition and culture. That in some communities grey hair and loss of teeth meant older members of the community had lived and learned and survived. Grey hair and loss of teeth and the ceremonial scars meant survival, and respect.

Nonno doesn't have any scars. Not ceremonial ones anyway. But he does wear dentures, so he's lost all his teeth. And his head only has a handful of hair left.

But he does have his medal. The medal Nonno has kept for so long.

During these past few years my nonno has probably forgotten more than I will ever know.

If I'm lucky, one day I'll be an old man just like The Don. Can't imagine myself all wrinkly, though. Maybe facelifts for guys will be really cool by then. And hopefully by then I'll have earned the right to some respect too.

I think of Nonno's aftershave bottles as I walk. He collected every one of them, from people like me, and Nonna Romina, and probably Dad too. People he loves, and who know how important it is for Nonno to always smell nice. Not to smell like goats. Those bottles link his present to his past, and I destroyed them.

But you can't ever destroy the past. You can stop remembering it as it actually was, but you can't destroy it, or change it. Not even Nonno can do that.

It's strange, though. All these years sharing the same bedroom, and I know so little about Nonno's aftershave bottles. I mean, I don't know who gave him which one, or why, or even if he didn't just buy them all himself. One day, soon, I'll have to sit Nonno down and get him to tell me as much as he can remember about them, even (especially) the ones I broke.

I remember Nonno's face as he looked at the shattered mess of glass outside our bedroom window. Hollow. That was his look. I know that feeling. It's how I sometimes feel about Dad.

We're so alike, Nonno and me. The Dons. That's us.

No, Mum and me won't let Nonno be put in a

home. We can still look after him, even if he does tell the neighbours they smell, even if he does think I should give a girl sheep.

It's Monday. Mum will be at work all morning and Nonno will be at the Italian Club. The council mini-bus would have picked him up just after I left for school this morning, and I can see Mum telling the driver to make certain Nonno gets back on the bus after lunch for the ride home, and that he's not to let Nonno sweet-talk him into letting him walk home alone.

Mondays and Wednesdays are card days at the Club. Wednesday is also bocce day for the men and crafts for the women. Friday is left for guest speakers and entertainers. Nonno loves Mondays, puts up with Wednesdays, and hates Fridays. Unless the entertain-ment involves a good-looking woman in a short skirt.

I look at my watch. I bolt. If I'm quick I can get to the Club before Nonno starts his card game. He hates being interrupted once the game's underway.

I've been to the Monday Club with Nonno before so I know how to get to it. I find Nonno there with three other wrinklies.

Nonno frowns uncertainly when he sees me at his elbow. 'You mama in the jail again?' he asks.

The men at the table stare at me. I know them by sight only and I nod my head and try a feeble smile.

'Hims mama is got police boyfriend,' Nonno adds

into the middle of the table. 'They like go to the jail.'
He is shuffling a deck of cards.

'I need your help with something,' I say and rest
both hands on the back of Nonno's chair. His walking-
stick is leaning against the table as usual. I nudge it
towards him.

'You need go look for the sheepsdog?' Nonno asks,
then smiles at the other men and adds, 'Hims got ghel
wot hims like name of Tratcy.'

'Yeah, something like that.' I wait for Nonno to put
down the deck of cards.

'Why you not at the school?' Nonno asks suddenly.
'Is holiday time already?' Then to the man on his left,
'Too much holiday dis country. Is good ting maibe,
maibe no.' The man blinks non-committally. 'Hims
going to be Pope!' Nonno announces, grinning in my
direction. 'Hims mama say for him go to Vatican for
be Pope.'

The men laugh. Nonno grins.

'*You* were going to be the Pope, remember?' I say.

Nonno pulls his face into a tight knot. For a
moment I think I've said something to hurt him. I'm
about to apologise when Nonno pushes back his chair
and reaches for his walking-stick. 'We is Ostraliano
people,' Nonno announces. 'If I wos be Pope I wos
never be Ostraliano people because I wos be in Rome.
I wos not be come to dis country. Maibe, Paul, you can
be Ostraliano Pope.'

The men laugh again and the man on Nonno's left reaches for the deck of cards Nonno has left on the table.

Nonno doesn't ask why he has to come with me, not even when I clear it with the lady in charge. Not even when I tell the man in charge of getting Nonno home on the minibus that Nonno's going to be with me and not to worry about having to drive him home today.

'We not need Porsche today!' Nonno says when we're out in the bright sunshine. 'We not even need Ferrari. Is not rain today, I tink.'

I look at Nonno. He's somewhere else. But for the first time in ages I don't mind. I don't mind at all. Sure, taking Nonno to school is a risk. A huge risk. He could go right off about nothing at all. But it's a risk I'm going to take. It's a risk *worth* taking.

A case of better late than never. The Don finally has his moment in the spotlight. His nephew, future Formula 1 racing ace, Paul 'The Don II' Taranto explains why he's so proud of his nonno.

'My teacher, Miss Wildermere, she wants you to visit my English class and show my class your medal,' I tell Nonno as we begin our walk towards home. 'She'd like you to sing for the class, if you don't mind too much. I thought maybe you could take your accordion and sing that song you learnt for the competition back in Monte Sereno when you were about my age.'

I feel Nonno hesitate.

'Something wrong?' I ask, my voice tinny because I'm afraid Nonno might tell me off.

'I can remember much clear that song,' Nonno announces. 'Is not sad song. Him not make you want cry.'

'Good, it's not a crying day today,' I answer in case Nonno wants to add something else. And because I'm trying hard to convince myself that Tracey Reynolds really isn't worth crying over.

Nonno mumbles something under his breath to cut me off and we move on.

'I like tell Tratcy about goats and sheeps in my village, and why hims is important,' Nonno says finally. 'You tink him likes hear about goats and sheeps?'

'Goats and sheep? Sure you can tell her about the goats and sheep. You can tell her about the cigarettes too, if you want. You can even talk about the Porsche. Tell her about the aftershave bottles, too.' I pause. 'Actually, maybe I'll tell them about your aftershave bottles,' I add. 'I think I know enough about them to do that.'

'And my medal? And my beautiful music? You really want I should talk of him?'

I look at The Don and smile. 'Sure,' I say. 'Absolutely.'

The Don grins and nods, takes out a handful of pistachio nuts and hands me a few. Then we walk on without saying another word. We don't want to be late for Lady Fang's class.

About the author

Archimede Fusillo was born in Melbourne to Italian immi-
grants. Since completing a Bachelor of Arts and Honours
degree in Psychology at the University of Melbourne, he
has worked as a teacher and features writer for two interna-
tional magazines. Many of Archimede's short stories have
been published in Australia's leading magazines and jour-
nals, and he has won several awards for his work, including
the Alan Marshall Award and the Mary Grant Bruce Award
for Children's Literature. He has also published several
textbooks for students and teachers.

Archimede Fusillo's concerns about traditions being lost
in the modern world, and about grandparents and their
stories disappearing, formed the basis for Paul and
Nonno's story in *The Dons*.

Archimede lives with his wife, Pina, and their two children, Alyssa and Laurence, in Melbourne's outer suburbs.
His first novel, *Sparring with Shadows*, was published in
1997 and was nominated in the Literature Category of the
prestigious Italy in the World Awards, 2000.

Also by Archimede Fusillo

David Martinesi is a first-generation Italian Australian growing up in an inner-city suburb. He is fighting the shadows cast by his Italian upbringing, and this summer he is quietly waiting for change.

Change comes when he is befriended by confident, street-wise Nathan. But tragedy comes too . . .

This is Archimede Fusillo's first novel – engaging, page-turning and moving. Nominated in the Literature Category of the Italy in the World Awards, 2000.

Also available from Penguin Books

Hannah would much rather be back in Australia starting secondary school with her friends than going to Japan. But Hannah's stay turns out to be nothing like she'd imagined, and when she and Miki find an ancient message in the stationery shop, they are drawn into solving a mysterious riddle.

Full of intriguing, vivid characters, here is a highly original, evocative debut novel that blends fact with fantasy in a style that is both funny and touching.

Also available from Penguin Books

Poor Bruno – as soon as his mysterious Great Aunt Ilma arrives with her musical instrument, he finds himself signed up for crumhorn lessons. Bruno can think of nothing worse, but no one asked his opinion and somehow he didn't have the courage to protest.

Still, if Bruno had refused, then he would never have met the exotic Early Musicians and, most importantly, he would never have met Sybil. . .

Also available from Penguin Books

GILLIAN RUBINSTEIN

Terra-FARMA

The long-awaited sequel to the highly acclaimed, award-winning *Galax-Arena*.

On the run from the all-seeing, all-knowing Project Genesis Five, Joella and Liane find shelter at Terra-Farma, while Peter tries to survive in the outback. But Terra-Farma is not what it seems. Can the girls escape again?

A sequel that equals *Galax-Arena* in its power to enthral the reader and challenge the way we think about the world.

Come exploring at

www.penguin.com.au

and

www.puffin.com.au

for

Author and illustrator profiles

Book extracts

Reviews

Competitions

Activities, games and puzzles

Advice for budding authors

Tips for parents

Teacher resources